ALL MEN
ARE LIARS

ALBERTO MANGUEL

Translated by Miranda France

ALMA BOOKS

ALMA BOOKS LTD
London House
243–253 Lower Mortlake Road
Richmond
Surrey TW9 2LL
United Kingdom
www.almabooks.com

First published in Spanish as *Todos los hombres son mentirosos* in 2008
This English translation first published by Alma Books Ltd in 2010
Copyright © Alberto Manguel
c/o Guillermo Schavelzon & Asoc., Agencia Literaria
www.schavelzon.com
Translation © Miranda France, 2010

Cover design: Nathan Burton

Work published within the framework of "Sur" Translation Support
Program of the Ministry of Foreign Affairs, International Trade and
Worship of the Argentine Republic

Supported by the National Lottery through Arts Council England

LOTTERY FUNDED

Printed in Great Britain by TJ International, Padstow, Cornwall

ISBN: 978-1-84688-109-1

CONTENTS

To Craig Stephenson,
who never lies

ALL MEN ARE LIARS

"I said in my haste, All men are liars."
Psalm 116:2

1

APOLOGIA

> "What of a truth that is bounded by these mountains and is falsehood to the world that lives beyond?"
>
> Michel de Montaigne
> *An Apology for Raymond Sebond*

Frankly, I'm the last person you should be asking about Alejandro Bevilacqua. What can I tell you, my dear Terradillos, about someone I haven't seen for thirty years? I mean, I hardly knew him, or if I did, then it was only very vaguely. To be honest, I didn't want to know him any better. Or rather: I *did* know him well – I admit that now – but only in a distracted sort of way – reluctantly, as it were. Our relationship (for want of a better word) had an element of courteous formality to it, as well as that conventional nostalgia shared among expatriates. I don't know if you understand. Fate threw us together, so to speak, and if you asked me now, hand on heart, if we were friends, I would have to confess that we had nothing in common, apart from the words *República Argentina* stamped in gold letters on our passports.

What draws you to this man, Terradillos? Is it the manner of his death? Is it that image – which still haunts my dreams even though I didn't see it with my own eyes – of Bevilacqua lying on the pavement, skull crushed, blood running down the street to the drain, as though wanting to flee from his lifeless body, as though refusing to be a part of such an abominable crime, of such an unjust, unforeseen ending?

I think not. You are a journalist, in love with life. You're a man of the pulsing world, I'd say, not an obituaries junkie. Far from it. It's the truth you're after, the living proof. You want to lay these facts before your readers, though they may not be much interested in someone like Bevilacqua, a man whose roots once delved into the soil of Poitou-Charentes (which, let us not forget, is your region too, Terradillos). You want your readers to know the truth – a dangerous concept if ever there was one. You hope to redeem Bevilacqua even as he lies in the grave. You want to equip him with a new biography assembled from other people's memories. And all this for the earth-shattering reason that Bevilacqua's mother hailed from the same corner of the world as you. It's a lost cause, my friend! Do you know what I suggest? Find another personality

– some colourful hero or notorious celebrity – of whom Poitou-Charentes can be really proud, like that heterosexual faggot Pierre Loti or that inquisitive egghead, Michel Foucault, darling of Yankee universities. You're good at writing learned articles, Terradillos, I can tell, and I know about these things. Don't waste your time on dross, or the hazy recollections of an ageing curmudgeon.

And, to return to my first question: why me?

Let's see. I was born at one of the many staging posts of a prolonged exodus, one that took my Jewish family from the Asiatic steppes to the steppes of South America; the Bevilacquas, by contrast, travelled straight from Bergamo to what would become the Province of Santa Fé towards the end of the eighteenth century. In that remote colony, those adventurous Italian settlers established a slaughterhouse; to commemorate their bloody achievement, in 1923 the mayor of Venado Tuerto bestowed the name Bevilacqua on one of the minor streets of the eastern zone. Bevilacqua *père* met the girl who would become his wife, Marieta Guittón, at a patriotic celebration; they were married within a few months. When Alejandro was a year old, his parents were killed in the rail disaster of 1939, and his paternal grandmother decided to take the boy to Buenos Aires, where she opened a delicatessen.

Bevilacqua (who, as you know, was annoyingly fastidious about details) once made a point of telling me that the family's business had not always been in tripe and cold cuts, and that, centuries ago, back in Italy, a Bevilacqua had been surgeon to the court of some cardinal or bishop. Señora Bevilacqua took pride in those vague but distinguished roots, preferring to ignore the Huguenot Guittóns. She was what we used to call a font-kisser, and I believe that in seventy years she never missed a day's Mass, until the heart attack that left her crippled.

My friend Terradillos, you think that I can paint you a portrait of Bevilacqua that is at once spirited, heartfelt and true to life; that you can pour my words straight onto the page, adding a dash of Poitiers colour. But that is precisely what I cannot do. Bevilacqua certainly trusted me; he confided in me some very personal details of his life, filling my head with all kinds of intimate nonsense, but, truth be told, I never understood why he was telling me all these things. I can assure you that I did nothing to encourage him – on the contrary. Perhaps he saw in me, his fellow countryman, a solicitude that wasn't there, or he decided to interpret my evident lack of affection as pragmatism. One thing's for sure: he turned up at my house at all hours of the day and night – oblivious to my work or my need to earn a living – and he'd start talking about the past, as though this flow of words, of *his* words, could recreate for him a world that, in spite of everything, he knew or felt to be irredeemably lost. It would have been pointless to protest that I did not share his condition of exile. I had left Argentina when I was ten years younger than him, a teenager yearning to travel. After putting down tentative roots in Poitiers, I moved on to Madrid, hoping it would be a good place to write, shouldering some of that resentment that Argentines inevitably feel towards the capital of the Mother Country while never actually surrendering to the commonplace of living in San Sebastián or Barcelona.

Don't take these observations the wrong way: Bevilacqua was not one of those people who plant themselves on your couch and then can't be shifted. On the contrary, he seemed incapable of the slightest rudeness, and that was what made it was so hard to ask him to leave. Bevilacqua possessed a natural grace, a simple elegance, an understated presence. Tall and slim, he moved slowly, like a giraffe. His voice was both husky and calming. His heavy-lidded eyes – typically Latin, in my opinion – gave him a sleepy appearance, and they fixed on you in such a manner that it was impossible to look away when he was talking to you. And when he reached to grab at your sleeve with those fine, nicotine-stained fingers, you let yourself be grabbed at, knowing that any resistance would be futile. Not until the time came to say goodbye would I realize that he had led me to waste a whole afternoon.

Perhaps one of the reasons why Bevilacqua felt so at home in Spain – even more so in those grey years – was that his imagination favoured dreams over concrete reality. In Spain – I don't know if you agree – everything has to be made obvious: they put signs on every building, plaques on every monument. Of course people who really know that pretentious village perceive Madrid as something else, semi-hidden, mysterious; the plaques are deceptive, and what the tourists see is simply a *mise-en-scène*. For some strange reason, he gave more credence to the shadowy evidence before him than to the substance of his own memories and dreams. Even though he had suffered, for decades, from political fabrications and press deception in our own country, he placed a surprising faith in the press fabrications and political deception of his adopted country, arguing that the former had been a pack of lies but that these were truths.

Do you see what I mean? Bevilacqua made a distinction between true falsehood and false truth. Did you know that he had a passion for documentaries, the drier the better? Before I knew that he was going to publish a novel, I never would have guessed that he had any talent for writing fiction, because he was the only person I knew who was capable of spending a night watching one of those films that follow a day in an Asturian meat-processing plant, or a sanatorium in the Basque mountains.

Now, don't go imagining that I did not think highly of him. Bevilacqua was – let me find the *mot juste* – very *sincere*. If he gave you his word, you felt obliged to take it, and it would never occur to you that this might be an empty gesture or mere formality. He was like one of those men I used to see as a boy in Buenos Aires – thin as a pencil, dressed in double-breasted suits, their black hair glossy with brilliantine beneath their Shabbat hats – who used to greet my mother as we walked to market. My mother (who knew about these things) said that these men's tongues were so clean that one could find out whether or not a coin was made of silver by placing it in their mouths: if it was false, it turned black from the slightest contact with their saliva. I think that my mother, who was a harsh judge of people, would have taken one look at Bevilacqua and declared him mensch. He had something of the provincial gentleman, Alejandro Bevilacqua, an unruffled air and an absence of guile which meant that one toned down jokes in his presence and tried to be accurate about anecdotes. It's not that the man lacked imagination, but rather that he had no talent for fantasy. Like St Thomas, the Apostle, he needed to touch what he saw before he could believe it was real.

That is why I was so surprised the night he turned up at my house and said he'd seen a ghost.

Where was I? Those countless mornings, afternoons and nights that I spent listening to Bevilacqua drone on about dull episodes in his life – watching him smoke cigarette after cigarette, rolling them between amber fingers, crossing and uncrossing his legs then jumping to his feet and taking great strides around my room – have merged in my memory into one single, monstrous day inhabited exclusively by this emaciated man. My memory, though increasingly unreliable, is both precise and vague on this point. I mean that it does not consist of a series of clear recollections, but in an agglomeration of brief, confused memories that seem contaminated by literature. I think that I am remembering Bevilacqua, but then portraits of Camus, or of Boris Vian, come to mind.

These days I share Bevilacqua's greyish hue, if not his emaciation. Inconceivably, I have aged; I have grown fat. He, on the other hand, seems as old as he was when I first met him: today we would say "young", but in those days it was "mature". I have continued, as it were, the story which we began together, or which Bevilacqua began, in an Argentina which is no longer ours. I know the chapters that followed his death (I was going to say his "disappearance", but that word, my friend Terradillos, we must not use). He of course, knows nothing of all that. What I mean is that the story he wove and picked apart so many times is now mine. I am the one who will decide his fate, who will make sense of his journey. That is the survivor's duty: to tell, to recreate, to invent – why not? – other people's stories. Take any number of events in the life of a man, distribute them as you see fit, and you will be left with a character who is unarguably real. Distribute them in a slightly different way and – *voilà!* – the character changes, it's a different person altogether, though equally real. All I can tell you is that I will devote the same care to my story of Alejandro Bevilacqua's life as I would wish a narrator to devote to my own, when the time comes.

I realize that we're not talking about a self-portrait here. It isn't Alberto Manguel you're interested in. A brief excursion into that tributary will be necessary, however, if we are going to navigate the main river with confidence. I promise not to drag the depths of my own waters, or to linger on its banks. But I need to explain some shared experiences, and in order to do that a few asides are necessary.

On one of the occasions you interviewed me, Terradillos, I believe I told you how it was that I came to live in Madrid, in the mid-Seventies, renting two small rooms at the top of the Calle del Prado. I had an American scholarship, and enjoyed the sort of robust health one cannot take for granted after thirty. I spent nearly a year and a half there, believe it or not, before events forced me to flee and take refuge here, in Poitiers. At the time, you asked me why I had chosen Poitiers. I'll answer you now: because I had to leave Madrid, a city that was haunted, for me, by the ghost of Alejandro Bevilacqua. Everything has changed since that time, and these days the city is full of music and light. But on the few occasions that I've returned, even when sitting at a café on the Paseo de la Castellana or the Plaza de la Ópera, I've felt his presence beside me, his fingers on my arm, the smell of tobacco in my nostrils, the cadence of his voice in my ears. I don't know if Madrid is particularly prone to such enchantments. You and I know that nothing like that ever happens in Poitiers.

It's strange, but sometimes I cannot be absolutely sure whether a certain memory is mine or his. Here's an example: Bevilacqua spoke fondly of the house in Belgrano, where he had lived with his paternal grandmother. I also lived in that neighbourhood, with its austere houses and streets lined with jacaranda trees, about seven or eight years after Bevilacqua had moved downtown. Now I no longer know if the house I half-remember is mine, or the one described to me by Bevilacqua, with its coloured-glass door panels, its narrow stairways, the velvet curtain separating the dining area from the sitting room, the chandelier reflected on the mahogany table, the bookcase with its blue volumes of *A Children's Treasury*, the porcelain figures of the Meissen monkey orchestra, in powdered wigs, playing a silent concert. It may even be an invented house, based on memories that are partly his and partly mine, but I'll never know now, because the neighbourhood has been torn down to make room for skyscrapers. It would have mattered to Bevilacqua, who was precise even about the detail of his dreams. It doesn't matter to me.

Bevilacqua believed that he had inherited this obsession with detail from his grandmother, a severe and demanding woman – here in Europe they would say she was not so much Catholic as Lutheran. Throughout Alejandro's infancy, his grandmother had reminded him that God is always watching us, day and night, with an unblinking eye, and that every gesture, every thought, is registered in his Great Book of Accounts, like the one that lay on the desk in the delicatessen. Ever faithful to her convictions, Señora Bevilacqua ran her business with exemplary rigour and hygiene, never allowing herself to be seduced by the new wave of supermarkets which were replacing shops like hers with plastic shelving and neon lights. La Bergamota, until well into the 1970s, was the pride of Belgrano.

She was equally rigorous with her grandson. Privations, prohibitions and lashings with the carpet-beater were alternated with rewards and affection. On one occasion, some adolescent nonsense got him locked in his room for three whole days, with nothing more than bread and water to eat or drink. Bevilacqua assured me that this was not an exaggeration: he literally got a slice of bread three times a day and a jug of tap water. There was something medieval about Señora Bevilacqua, something of the embittered, unyielding dowager, with a touch of the overseer.

And yet, in spite of Señora Bevilacqua's avowed desire that her grandson follow the family tradition, he never felt that his destiny lay among sausages and cheese. After school, before entering the shop redolent of brine, where he helped his grandmother to fish ladlefuls of olives out of the oak barrels, or to turn the handle on the ham-slicing machine, Bevilacqua used to stop in front of the bookshop (at least that's what I imagine), where the yellow volumes of the

Robin Hood series were displayed in the window, and dream of faraway countries and extraordinary encounters. He imagined himself a Sandokan or a Phileas Fogg, but those distant lands were no further than the Tigre Delta, just outside Buenos Aires, and his Indian princess was the pharmacist's daughter. Later he realized that he was drawn not so much by the lure of journeys and adventures, but simply by things that appear out of reach.

When did I first see him? In Madrid, in February or March of 1976, at the offices of Quita, our go-between and our nemesis.

Blanca, Blanquita, Blanquita Grenfeld. Larralde de Grenfeld. Always elegant, always bright, always on the crest of the *nouvelle vague*. Of course you know who I'm talking about! Oh, Terradillos! Fame works in mysterious ways! In Argentina, before the dictatorship, Blanquita Grenfeld was the supreme ruler in the world of culture. She was the younger daughter of the Larraldes, landowners who lost everything in a failed enterprise to raise yaks – or was it camels? – on the pampa. As dark as a mulatta, she was married in her teens to some German industrialist – who was considerate enough to die shortly afterwards – leaving her to enjoy a widowhood that liberated her simultaneously from a groping parent and a dim-witted husband. Blanca

Larralde de Grenfeld used the name of her incestuous father and the fortune of the deceased industrialist to establish her own republic of Arts and Literature. In Buenos Aires, no painting was hung, no book published, no film shown or play put on without her say-so. Everyone, from the most bureaucratic official to the most anarchic artist, knew her as "Quita". She was present at every creation. She was also one of the first to leave. "Let's go and make culture in the motherland," Quita said, when the military began to close down bookstores and raid theatres and galleries.

A few weeks after moving to Madrid, Quita founded the Casa Martín Fierro, on a fourth floor in the Prospe district, among bungalows and workers' houses. There, like some refined materfamilias, she played host to the fugitives, the born-again, the dispossessed, the damaged, the lost and found that the various dictatorships of Latin America had not yet contrived (and please forgive the transitive use of the verb) to "disappear". She looked gorgeous in her suit and pearls, a leopard-skin coat thrown over her shoulders like a cape, an aristocratic down on her upper lip and her eyes always lively behind tortoiseshell glasses. She had the right words for everyone, without that undertow of contempt that so often accompanies philanthropy. Behind the desk in the reception area, a brand-new bookcase displayed a copy of the immortal *Martín Fierro*, by Hernández, various books that had been banned by the military regime and a couple of *matés* which Andrea, Quita's loyal assistant, had learnt to offer the guests. From that time on, no refugee arrived in Spain without stopping off to present their credentials at Quita's place.

The telephone rang one morning when I was thinking of catching up on one of those big backlogs of sleep that are the privilege of youth. It was Quita.

"Come over immediately."

Without opening my eyes, I asked where to.

"To the Martín Fierro, of course."

I said that I didn't understand. Quita heaved an impatient sigh. There was a newly arrived group of Argentines who needed our help. That "we", for reasons I did not fully understand, included me. And I admit that I felt flattered. Quita was calling on me. Ergo, I existed.

She explained that one of the refugees appeared to be a writer.

"A novelist," she added. "The surname's Bevilacqua. He's very good-looking. Do you know him?"

I said that I did not. The truth was that, since I had left Buenos Aires, I wasn't very up-to-date with Argentine writing. With youthful arrogance I judged that if this Bevilacqua had published something in the last two or three years, his books must obviously be either official propaganda or pseudo-romantic pap.

"We're due a renaissance," I added, but Quita had already hung up.

When I arrived at the Martín Fierro, Bevilacqua was installed in a tiny chair, but with all the dignity of a man seated on a throne. When he saw me, he got to his feet.

He was the saddest person I had ever seen. The others who were with him, two or three new arrivals, looked at me like dogs in a pound; by comparison, they seemed merely tired. That melancholy that afflicts most *porteños* manifested itself physically in Bevilacqua's whole body. He was someone who suffered – that was obvious – but in such a visceral and profound way that it was impossible for him to contain the sadness: it darkened his appearance, stooped his shoulders, softened his features. It withered him to such a degree that it was difficult to gauge how old he was. If one tried to touch him, he shrank away. Through goodness knows which diplomatic stratagems, he had been pulled out of prison only two days earlier and put on a plane with hardly any luggage.

As though to justify my presence, Quita explained that I was a writer and a fellow Argentinian. For the sake of saying something, I mumbled a question about what books he had published. For the first time, Bevilacqua smiled.

"No, brother," he answered. "It's not books I write. I used to make fotonovelas for a living."

Perhaps I should explain, Terradillos, what these fotonovelas are, because I'm guessing that this form of literature is not popular in France. Back in the 1930s, some long-forgotten genius thought to combine the attractions of movies, comic strips and romantic novels, thereby inventing a new hybrid genre between drama and photography. Actors were positioned as required, photographed at different angles, and then speech bubbles with the relevant dialogue were superimposed on the photographs. Bevilacqua penned the contents of those bubbles.

Quita was not to be defeated.

"That also counts as art," she said later, when we were alone. "Don't tell me that we're only going to help people who write high literature. My conditions of acceptance are the same as those of the Real Academia: it's sufficient for him to know that there's no 'h' in España. Manguel, don't be a shit. This man needs our help."

"A new favourite," some onlooker observed as, after wishing Bevilacqua luck and giving him my address, I said goodbye with a hug. "It's the same everywhere."

Two days later, in the middle of the afternoon, Bevilacqua turned up at my house, shivering with cold. Thus began the first of many such afternoons.

Of course you probably want to know all the details of Bevilacqua's early life: the ins and outs of his primary education, his sexual initiation, his first steps in politics, his imprisonment and torture. And again I must say that I am not the best person to answer these questions. Discretion, if not indifference, was our watchword during those months in which we used to see each other. I know what you're thinking: he talked and I resigned myself to listening, and you imagine that, out of that farrago I must have salvaged some dramatic scene, some crucial episode. It wasn't like that. Bevilacqua would talk about his life in an erratic way, filling an improvised ashtray with yellow cigarette butts, with no concern for the historical or chronological coherence of his tale. This was no Bildungsroman he was spinning me, but something more akin to a story from one of his fotonovelas – predictable, melodramatic and doomed.

Let us take, as an example, that Buenos Aires he remembered through a haze of nostalgia. Bevilacqua could not believe that I didn't miss the city – which, I believe, is better in memories than in real life. Bevilacqua, in contrast, not only missed the place in which he had lived; he missed the very map of Argentina. I mean, he missed the forests, the mountains, the great expanses of plains which he could have seen only once or twice – if that – from a train. I, in contrast, was drawn to ever smaller space: a market square rather than the countryside; a village rather than the city. Madrid and Poitiers, as you well know, are villages with a metropolitan vocation. Bevilacqua suffered from what you French call *le mal du pays* – but I think he'd still have had it, even if it had been possible for him to return. He was missing not a place, but a moment that had passed, a geography of lost hours in streets that no longer existed, where he had lingered in the doorways of houses long since demolished, or in cafés which had some time ago exchanged their *boiserie* and marble for glass panels and formica. Believe me, I understood his nostalgia – I just didn't share it.

For me, Buenos Aires was a city in which I had scarcely lived and which – even during the years that I knew it – had entered a decline. Bevilacqua, on the other hand, had fallen in love with Buenos Aires when she was still a *grande dame*, resplendent in silk and high heels, perfumed and bejewelled, unaffectedly elegant and unostentatiously brilliant. But in the last few decades (this was how Bevilacqua explained recent Argentine history), a shameful illness had defiled her. She had lost her grace, her eloquence.

Her new avenues and skyscrapers seemed false, like artificial limbs. Her gardens were withering; a dense fog descended on her, one that was barely pierced by the intermittent glow of orange lamplights. By comparison with this decayed Buenos Aires, the city of his childhood seemed a thousand times more beautiful and radiant.

From very early on, when he first became aware of a certain subcutaneous itch and of a particular weight in the groin, he knew that what he felt for Buenos Aires was similar to an erotic attraction. To touch the rough stone façades, the cold railings, to smell the jasmin in September and the damp pavements in March (I too was in Paradise!) aroused him. Walking down the street where he lived or sitting on the plastic seats in the buses made him pant and sweat with desire.

"*Souvenir, souvenir, que me veux-tu,*" as someone once said. I've remembered something that may satisfy your scurrilous, journalistic curiosity.

Bevilacqua first fell in love on the day of his twelfth birthday. A classmate oddly named Babar (which is why I've never forgotten him) had told him about a cinema a few blocks away from the Retiro station, wedged into the wall which separated the tracks from the Paseo Colón. The woman in the box office didn't ask if the boy with the unconvincingly deep voice was indeed eighteen, as required by the notice at the entrance. With his blood pounding in his ears, Bevilacqua penetrated the gloom and groped his way towards a seat. Incidentally, the cinema smelled of sweat and ammonia.

Bevilacqua could never remember (if indeed he ever knew) the name of the film: he thought that it was German or Swedish, and he never saw it again. The storyline, so he told me, sparing no details, had something to do with a country girl who went off to the city to seek her fortune. This innocent child had a heart-shaped face and wore a tight white dress which, in the film's raunchiest scene, she tore off and flung onto a chair. Bevilacqua watched on, mesmerized, as her face filled the screen and a boy (because of course there was a boy) kissed her. With mawkish sentimentality, Bevilacqua told me that he had felt as though the lips kissing her were his own.

Gradual fade-out. The following scene showed dawn breaking over the tiled rooftops. Naked but for a pair of underpants, the boy jumped out of bed and started to fry a couple of eggs. The girl asked him sleepily if it wasn't too early to eat eggs. Bevilacqua, for whom breakfast, in the Argentine style, consisted only of coffee and toast, never forgot the answer: "I eat what I want, when I want." "It was then," he told me, "that I understood what that freedom was that I had dreamt about in my grandmother's shop. Freedom was fried eggs at dawn."

I don't know if the poor man really believed in the relevance of this inane observation, or if he made it simply to relive the adventure – but it's certainly true that Bevilacqua spent a large part of his adolescence wanting to do unusual things in unpredictable places. For survival's sake, Bevilacqua meekly filled the roles required of him by convention – loyal grandson, disciplined student, restless adolescent – at the same time regarding himself as a youth far wiser than any adult authority, braver than any adventurer, and so bursting with passionate love that his imagination latched onto worldly knowledge like those sticky spider threads known in Argentina as "the devil's drool".

The heart-shaped face of that anonymous actress pervaded his dreams. I think that he must have superimposed her face onto every other woman's, even years after that first encounter. In his tedious descriptions her features changed, often depending on the context, so that sometimes the hair was black and silky like Loredana's, sometimes the eyes were smaller and shining like Graciela's, sometimes the whole face became translucent and hazy, as though it belonged to a woman in his memory who had almost vanished. He searched for that face throughout his adolescence. Once he thought he spotted it in one of those mildly pornographic magazines, *Rico Tipo*, or *Tutti Frutti*, which tend to pile up in the barber shops. After that, he started looking for her among the newpaper sellers of the Puente Saavedra, beneath the pillars of the Panamerican Highway. He never found her again.

You'll be wondering how I manage (in spite of reservations) to reproduce these conversations. I confess that during my time in Madrid, when I was not yet fat and my beard not yet white, it did cross my mind to write a novel. The thought of adding my own volume to the universal library was wickedly tempting – as it would be for any other person with a love of books. I had in mind a character, an artist, whose whole life would founder because of one lie. The novel would be set in Buenos Aires and – since I trust my memory more than my imagination – I told myself that these confidences of Bevilacqua's would come in useful for the creation of my fictional protagonist. Very soon, however, I realized that Bevilacqua's memories lacked passion and colour and, almost without thinking, I began to add to his stories a little fantasy and humour.

As I've said before, Bevilacqua was a stickler for details – which, as you know very well, is a way of avoiding emotion. He protected his secrets by wallowing in minutiae. Between one cigarette and the next, he would get to his feet to show me how the characters involved had behaved, using his saffron-coloured fingers to re-enact their gestures; he imitated their voices and gave me lists of names, dates, places. Such was his obsession with accuracy and his horror of getting things wrong that Bevilacqua gave the impression of reinventing his past, as though to convince me of its existence.

I don't know if I'm making myself clear, dear Terradillos. Nobody has a clear memory of events that happened years ago, unless he has had them photographed and archived for the purpose of reproducing them later. Apparently Balzac did that: he created faces for his characters, tried them out in front of the mirror, then sat down to describe them. It was the same for Bevilacqua. His descriptions of the people in his past were so sharp that I felt I had seen with my own eyes (for example) the little Lennon glasses that Babar wore, his military waistcoats and his contagious smile. When Bevilacqua was reminiscing, I kept quiet, not wanting to encourage him. But after he had gone, I was left with the feeling of having taken part in some sort of retrospective performance.

Bevilacqua admired people for whom the world was based on solid facts, on figures and documents. He did not believe in invention. He had discovered his mistrust in appearances very early on. I can put a date on it for you: it was a Sunday in September, after the inevitable Mass. Walking along behind his grandmother, Bevilacqua saw a scruffy old man standing beneath a jacaranda tree on the street corner. In his sermon on charity, the priest had described the archetypal beggar to whom St Martin of Tours gave half his cloak on a winter afternoon; this old man's bushy moustache and threadbare sleeves matched the description of the beggar in the sermon. Bevilacqua saw this apparition as proof of the power of reality, which had come to give substance to the priest's words. His response to that power was to take out a few coins from his pocket and place them in the shrivelled hand. The old man looked at the coins, looked at his benefactor and burst out laughing. Bevilacqua mumbled an explanation. Still laughing, the old man apologized, thanked him for the gesture and returned the coins.

For a few days afterwards, Bevilacqua looked for the old man he had seen on the corner of the street. Then, one afternoon, returning from school, he saw him standing, as before, beneath the same tree. The old man motioned for him to come forward. Bevilacqua obeyed, feeling a little nervous. Now that he saw him again, he was not too sure what to say. It was the old man who spoke first.

"You're wondering what I'm doing standing here on my own, looking like this, if I'm not a beggar, aren't you? You imagine that beggars look like this. You see me and say to yourself, 'that's a beggar'. But you shouldn't trust appearances, boy. Do you like puppets?"

Bevilacqua had seen a puppet show only once in his life, at a boring birthday party. Curiosity and surprise prompted him to say that he did.

"Follow me," said the apocryphal beggar and, taking the boy by his arm, he led him towards the Barrancas district. They stopped in front of a decrepit-looking house with large, low windows.

I'll paint the scene for you.

Bevilacqua had recently entered adolescence. Far from mistrusting the human libido, the interest which he was capable of provoking in adults intrigued him. That second glance in the bus; that silent sizing-up, seeking signs of mutual interest in the street; that knee moving closer in the darkness of a cinema – Bevilacqua took them as a compliment, as welcoming gestures on the threshold of adulthood. I'm not saying that the old man was a pervert, nor that Bevilacqua had a taste for those pleasures so well described in Greek literature. But something that he had not noticed before now removed his fear, prompting him to carry on, to go with the old man and slip into the rooms of an unknown house.

"Slip" is perhaps not the right word, since it suggests a progress which meets no resistance. The rooms of this house were obstacles in themselves, each one stuffed with all kinds of objects: wardrobes, shelves crammed with books, armchairs, desks and bedside tables, statues that looked as though they were made of stone and turned out to be papier-mâché, piles of newspapers tied together with twine, laundry baskets, unidentifiable packages – and on top of every object, protruding from every conceivable gap, there were puppets of every style and size. Arms, legs, daubed faces with glass eyes and colourful wigs peeped coyly out from behind the furniture or sprawled obscenely on the boxes, collectively evoking an orgy or a battlefield. For a few seconds, Bevilacqua had the impression of having entered an ogre's cave, filled with the corpses of dwarves.

The old man picked up a Roman soldier from a threadbare chair and offered the seat to Bevilacqua, then sat down opposite him, on a large painted chest. Apparently the old man (whose name, by the way, was Spengler) then launched into a long and seductive paean to the art of puppetry, in which creatures made of wood and felt enacted before an audience a more solid reality than that of our own illusory world. Spengler said that he took his theatre to schools and parks, factories and prisons, with the aim of telling what he called "truthful lies". "I am a missionary from the world of storytelling," he told Bevilacqua. And giving the boy a little slap on the thigh (Bevilacqua would have judged it innocent, but I'm not so sure), he began pulling on different strings, leaping over the furniture and making mysterious noises.

As you can imagine, Bevilacqua was fascinated by all those tiny arms and bodies, noses and eyes. At twelve or thirteen, we do not want anything to be strange, and yet strange things hold an irresistible attraction for us. They are appealing and terrifying at the same time. Bevilacqua was torn between going and staying. Just then, a girl – a woman, almost – came into the room and sat down at one of those cluttered tables to mend some of the puppets. Later Bevilacqua learnt that her name was Loredana.

Bevilacqua began to visit Don Spengler at all times of the day: as the years passed, he never lost that disagreeable habit of thinking that other people should tailor their day around his. He went to see him before school or in the evening, when Señora Bevilacqua was busy at La Bergamota. I imagine that the old man must have felt flattered: Bevilacqua was already blessed, it seems, with that seductive expression bestowed on him by hooded eyes, pronounced eyebrows and black irises. Spengler was not, however, the one he came to see, much though he had grown fond of the mustachioed old man. He came looking for Loredana, who barely even spoke to him as she bent over her mending, in a low-cut top, crossing her legs in such a way as to reveal one thigh, as shiny as an apple. He would find Spengler sleeping in an armchair with a book, or making his marionettes dance frenetically on an improvised dais, or staring out of the window, lost in thought, or painting, with brisk brushstrokes, a face or some scenery. Don Spengler seemed to move from an almost catatonic state to one of febrile activity, with no intermediate stages, and Bevilacqua used to make bets with himself about how he would find the old man on a given morning or afternoon.

Loredana was not always at home, but the mere fact of knowing that she had been there a few hours earlier or that she would be coming later – when he would already have gone – filled Bevilacqua at once with a sensation of anguish and dreaminess. When he did see her, he felt that Loredana handled the soldiers and princesses with the skill of a goddess. On the lips of Bevilacqua, that word was no mere hyperbole.

Now, if it had been up to me to invent a life for Bevilacqua, I would have gone about it differently. Knowing how he was when he arrived in Spain

– knowing, above all, about his tragic end and the terrible events that drove him to it – I would have furnished him with a more passionate childhood: skirmishes with the underworld, affairs with older women, some petty criminality which would later, towards the end of his adolescence, evolve into revolutionary action. Because, the way he himself told it, violence, frenzied love, politics (the kind which landed him in prison) played no more than chance roles in his life, were nothing but accidents of fate. Bevilacqua was cut out for observation, contemplation, like that traveller of Baudelaire's who cares about nobody – neither family nor friends – but only for the clouds: *les merveilleux nuages*.

It's my belief, Terradillos, that this contemplative vocation fostered his talent as a storyteller, for detailing trivialities with a pornographer's gusto. For example, Spengler only mattered as a preamble to Loredana, yet Bevilacqua claimed to remember the old man's entire life story.

It seems that Spengler had been born in Stuttgart, not far from the house of the philosopher Hegel (who had even exchanged greetings with his grandfather once or twice). His family was in the watchmaking business, and the regular ticking of clocks had inured them to the passage of time. Spengler's father was a devout but cantankerous Jew who spent his days ranting and raving about the iniquity of his God. He had devoted himself to clocks out of respect for the great mechanisms of Time, but without actually conceding them his approval. It struck him as scandalous that God should have invented a single, continuous, eternal time while simultaneously apportioning to men short little spans in which – adding insult to injury – there was nothing for them but frustration and suffering. His wife, who was dumpy and dumb, smiled all day and night while he, reddening with rage, bent over his wheels and cogs. "A man must keep on working," he muttered, "even when his employer is a madman."

At the age of twelve, Spengler was apprenticed to a puppet-maker, and never saw his parents again. War hounded him to the edge of the Atlantic. There his master, too exhausted to attempt the journey to the New World, gave him a trunk full of puppets together with a little money from his savings, and saw him off on a boat loaded with Syrians who had little clue where they were going. That was how he arrived in Buenos Aires, one autumn afternoon, thousands of years ago. He wanted Bevilacqua to know about his background, so as to understand that all human lives are, in the end, the same. "Directionless, difficult, incomprehensible," he told the boy, gently slapping his leg. "But the same."

I am, on principle, totally against giving psychological explanations, but – if you want my opinion – I do believe Bevilacqua felt that Spengler's presence settled, in some way, the debt of his own parents' death. He decided to devote his life to puppets. He would learn the necessary skills from the old man, and he would be with Loredana. Señora Bevilacqua (who was beginning to lose all notion of time and to forget people's names and faces) was persuaded to approve his increasingly long sessions at Spengler's place. Finally came the memorable day when the old man allowed him to work one of the puppets in public. Even years later, Bevilacqua could still sing to himself the music that was played when the curtain went up.

Let's talk about Loredana now. How often had he seen her? Half a dozen times at Spengler's, perhaps a few more in the street and at the little theatre. From those snippets, he had assembled an entire physical person. The English talk about "falling in love"; Bevilacqua would never have used such an expression. For Bevilacqua to become enamoured of someone was no accident, no happenstance: to love was to be converted, to acquire a new state of being. You did not fall in it, you let it fall over you, like rain, soaking you to the marrow. I don't know if Loredana realized that; I suppose she did – women know about these things. Loredana never gave him any encouragement. She was impeccably polite, allowing him to walk her to the bus stop, or to give her a box of candied fruit or a tin of La Gioconda *membrillo* stolen from his grandmother's shop – but she never confided in him or cracked a joke. Bevilacqua learnt nothing of her life beyond Spengler's workshop, on the other side of the curtain, except that Spengler had trained her himself and that her surname was Finnish.

A little before Christmas 1956, Don Spengler was invited by a producer of variety shows to put on a performance in Santiago, in Chile. Loredana, of course, was going to go with him. Bevilacqua fell into despair. I don't think he had told anyone about his feelings. He could never have confided such a thing to Señora Bevilacqua, and – as far as I know – he had only one real friend at school. All reality was reduced now to this one single fact and its consequences: Loredana was going. He would be left alone. He could not live without her. He decided to follow her.

You can imagine my surprise when he told me about this adolescent escapade. Nobody – certainly not I – would have thought of Bevilacqua as an impulsive person, a man of action. We used to talk (or rather he talked while I, as usual, kept an eye on my watch) about sudden and rash acts, the kind that people associate with a Latin temperament. Bevilacqua praised them. Not for him the cool, premeditated decision, but rather the one that strikes suddenly, like lightning. I think I told you before that I thought of Bevilacqua as very much a northern Italian – very rational. Perhaps he hoped that by telling me about this adventure, he would show me that he was not like that at all.

The greatest difficulty was crossing the border with Chile. He knew that his identity card would be enough, but he also knew that, as a minor, he would need his grandmother's authorization – and that she would never give it. The solution was to obtain a document from someone older. Reasoning that identity photographs are rarely recognizable, he persuaded Babar to get hold of his older brother's card – with the excuse that he wanted to get into some particularly smutty cabaret – and lend it to him for a few days. To get money, he sold his Grundig tape recorder to a neighbour's daughter. He bought a train ticket, packed a few scant belongings and left a note for Señora Bevilacqua very early one morning, in which he explained that he wanted to go out into the world and make his fortune, on his own and without asking anyone's help. He hinted that his adventure might take him to Patagonia –

which, for Señora Bevilacqua, had a reputation as fearsome as the Amazon jungle.

I don't know if you agree with me, Terradillos, but there is something magical about train journeys. Boarding a train at the start of a new life (or what Bevilacqua imagined to be a new life) must have felt like an epic moment for the boy. He noticed every detail, as if they were already passing into history: the cherry-coloured upholstery, the long-haired guard, a group of boys playing guitar. Everything was important, because each moment (so Bevilacqua told himself) was now part of his future.

He journeyed across a monotonous landscape for one interminable day; to Bevilacqua it seemed the necessary preparation for a great victory. When the mountains appeared, they confirmed his expectations. Before night fell, the train arrived at a little border station, tucked between stone walls and dirty snow. While they waited for the engine to be brought down the other side, Bevilacqua and the other passengers got out to stretch their legs on the platform, which was crowded half with Argentinians, half with Chileans. The oriental-looking officer cast an indifferent glance at Bevilacqua's apocryphal document. Years later, Bevilacqua would comment, as if it had just dawned on him: "I have walked on the Andes." The rest of the journey took place in darkness.

When he arrived in Santiago, it was after midnight. He must have fallen asleep because, when he got down from the train, the other passengers had disappeared. The station was deserted, and an old man was sweeping the platforms. As he emerged onto the street, he saw the gates being locked.

He had heard Don Spengler mention the name of the theatre where they were going to perform, and asked a taxi driver if it was far away. He set off walking. It was dark, of course, but finally he picked out the lights of the Gran Hotel O'Higgins, on the other side of the road. He went in and asked the receptionist if this was where Don Spengler and his troupe were staying. The receptionist said that it was. Bevilacqua asked to be put through to Loredana's room.

Let me say that when Bevilacqua claimed not to be a writer there was some truth in that. He lacked the inventive spark necessary for fiction, that disregard for what is and that excitement about what could be. He didn't imagine: he saw and documented things, which is not the same. Proust goes looking for details *a posteriori*, because he wants the past to confirm what he is inventing in the present. Not so Bevilacqua: he was interested in the *a priori*, in facts as pure narration, with no gloss, no commentary.

I don't know what he was expecting. That his beloved would cry out with joy, run downstairs and hurl herself into the arms of her intrepid Hannibal? That she would invite him into her bed, share the night with him as a reward for his bravery? I know that the last thing he expected was absolute silence. He heard the receiver being picked up, some sleepy breathing; he heard the echo of his own voice saying "Loredana, it's me, Alejandro"; he heard the receiver being put down. Still holding the handset, he asked the receptionist if there was a free room for the night. As the man got him a key, Bevilacqua heard himself observe that it was the first time he had ever stayed in a hotel.

That unbearable night finally reached its end. Bevilacqua had not slept a wink, as far as he remembered, but when he saw that it was light outside, he got up and went downstairs. Don Spengler was in the restaurant room, having breakfast on his own. Loredana had woken him and told him about what had happened. She had also told him to send Bevilacqua back to Buenos Aires that same morning. Bevilacqua refused. He had left everything to be with her. He would follow her wherever she went. He would love her in silence, from the shadows. He couldn't go back.

Don Spengler tried to persuade him. He repeated his lecture on reality and our obligation to accept it. But for Bevilacqua, the fiction, the lie, was Loredana's absence; the truth consisted in her accepting his presence, his act of love, his very self.

At that moment, Loredana entered the room. It took him a minute to recognize her. This Chilean Loredana was different. The one from his memory, his yearning, was taller, darker, marked by absence and desire. In every waking hour, every sleeping minute, he had felt Loredana's physical presence, from the brush of her hair against his arm to the scent of apples exuded by her skin under her clothes. This woman who came into the restaurant room was different: slightly round-shouldered, haggard, rather graceless in her movements. As though to confirm her presence, Bevilacqua tried to grasp her arm. Loredana avoided him, and was about to sit down when Bevilacqua once more put his hand out towards her. Loredana slapped him. Then Don Spengler got to his feet and ordered the girl to go to her room. Her suitor's nose was bleeding. Don Spengler handed him a napkin to wipe it. Bevilacqua turned to catch a final glimpse of her, but Loredana had already gone.

That very afternoon he returned to Buenos Aires, this time by plane, courtesy of Don Spengler. At the border, an official pored over his document, but let him through without saying anything. I don't know what explanation he may have given his grandmother. Years later, Bevilacqua still wished he could ask Loredana why she had not spoken to him. It was something that he never came to understand.

Bevilacqua told me that his grandmother did not ask him where he had been. He never knew for sure if she had read his note, or if she had simply decided to ignore something that would have been hard for her to understand. What was true was that, from that moment onwards, Señora Bevilacqua scarcely paid him any attention. Perhaps, in some way, after all the years of bickering and punishments, she had realized that force and discipline were of little avail where her grandson was concerned, and decided to take a kind of *laissez-faire* approach – that is, to let him live his life. It began to seem more important to Señora Bevilacqua (less bewildering you might say) not to leave two knives crossed on a table, for this presaged a fight, than to ask her grandson for a truthful account of his life out in the big world.

In the only photograph that Alejandro possessed of his grandmother (which, of course, he showed to me), Señora Clara Bevilacqua was pictured in black and white – a thin, pale woman, her eyebrows plucked and drawn in, as though with a violet pencil, her hair arranged in tight curls, as rigid as a jockey's helmet. Wearing a flowery dress, and posed against a chalk wall, she bore an expression of unflinching hardship. She was tall, upright and severe, a woman who was clearly uncomfortable with physical contact and didn't go in for hugs and kisses. Throughout his childhood, Bevilacqua felt that he must have failed some secret test. He never knew which, but this mystery and his sense of failure made him feel guilty nonetheless. So Bevilacqua's adolescence passed between that ancient and haughty woman and the evanescent Loredana.

I must confess to a certain impatience with Bevilacqua's angst. All my life, my parents had believed that every single thing I did was the work of a genius, and that my faults were the mere peccadillos of a saint. Señora Bevilacqua held the opposite view: any task upon which her grandson embarked must, from the outset, be destined for failure. Without knowing it, this woman – just like my parents – was in the grip of superstitions that predate the cultures of the Po river or the Caucasus. For my parents, these simply constituted the rules of the game, whereas for Bevilacqua's grandmother, they were traps set by an imperious and vengeful God, traps that her hapless grandson would not know how to avoid. Poor Bevilacqua – I think that his grandmother never really loved him.

One thing was certain: when the boy returned from Chile, the world had changed, for his Loredana was no longer in it. Then he decided to alter his habits, his daily itinerary, as if to take revenge, through his own conduct, on the conduct of what he dared not call fate. His grandmother's life was divided between her home, the church and the shop. Bevilacqua wanted to escape from all three. He began to find excuses to linger after school, or to leave the house earlier than usual. Every day he took a different route to school, and he would lose himself in the tree-lined streets of the poorer neighbourhoods, in ancient parks, or among building complexes whose purpose he could not guess at. In those days, Buenos Aires was a good city to get lost in. Hours went by like this, and then weeks, months. It is strange how one afternoon can prolong itself to infinity, and several years be reduced to five words.

But I don't know if you're interested in this, Terradillos. I don't know if what I'm saying is at all useful. You want to know why Alejandro Bevilacqua died. You want to know how a polite and reasonable man in his forties, at a time when fortune was beginning to smile on him, came to grief against the pavement of the Calle del Prado, in the early hours of a Sunday in January, beneath my balcony.

I'm getting round to it, my friend. Be patient.

I have a theory about these things. We often think of our births as being the result of a chance series of historical and personal events, of the ebb and flow of society, as well as the personal circumstances of our own parents and grandparents – that is, to the tendril-like current of the world itself. But our deaths also stem from these comings and goings – perhaps even more so – and from circumstances both important and trivial. Just as our coming into the world is the result of many thousands of actions, both secret and public, so is our leaving it. In order to explain any death, especially a violent, mysterious death, it should be enough to carry out an exhaustive review of time, to retrieve every detail, every word, every avatar of that life, and then to wait for our intelligence to decipher the constellation formed from all these facts. Detectives must be partly astrologers. Poirot and Paracelsus are blood brothers. I've always said that a criminal investigation resembles the study of celestial bodies – at least it does in books, where all the greatest crimes are solved.

Let's start with the scene. Do you remember, or can you at least imagine, what Madrid was like then, in the mid-Seventies, when the stench, the darkness, the dejection of those years under the Caudillo were just beginning to fade away? I say "just", because there was still a sense of wandering through a lugubrious *ballo in maschera*, especially for someone young, as I was then, with the echo of real *porteño* parties still ringing in my ears. None of the faces were genuine

– they were all hiding something; each of them lied as a matter of course. The city itself wore a mask – it was a city in flight from itself, pretending not to feel that ubiquitous unease, that weight of sadness menacing from the shadows.

Because there was something else, and you could feel it. You knew that it was present on winter mornings, for example, when a dirty mist swirled through the streets of the city centre, around the Plaza de Oriente and into the squalid crannies of alleyways slithering like earthworms between the grimy brick houses. Or sometimes in the summer, when the rubbish that had accumulated in corners over the weekend filled the night with the putrid odour of artichokes and sour wine. Often, during the time I spent in Madrid, listening over and again to a recording of 'Bohemian Rhapsody' a friend had sent from New York, I felt as if I were suffocating.

In my room on the Calle del Prado, I would some-times glance up from my writing to see people in funereal garb advancing wearily, as though dragged along by a river of mud. Only when I saw a couple – he wearing blue, she wearing red – running up the street laughing, did I begin to feel that change was in the air.

To the South Americans, on the other hand, coming from where they came, Madrid was like a dream. True, the new culture that people said was being forged in France, in Italy, in England (even in Sweden – imagine that!), was not much in evidence here, but neither did they live in constant fear of a kidnapping, an interrogation. If this new land seemed like a desolate place where no one – not even the vermin – could be bothered to create anything, the cities from which they had fled were wastelands where even inactivity was dangerous, where every crack was suspicious, every stone a threat. Buenos Aires, Montevideo and Santiago were barren and frightening places, whereas Madrid, as far as they were concerned, was simply reassuringly barren. I know a number of writers who lugged half-finished books inside bulky folders with them into exile. They managed to finish them in Barcelona, in San Sebastián, even in Seville. Not in Madrid.

Enrique Vila-Matas got interested in this phenomenon I'm describing to you, that of the exiled, unwritten novel. Vila-Matas met Bevilacqua during those years (if only you had seen him then – the future author of *Montano's Malady*, such an elegant young dandy, a connoisseur of fine wines and fine women!), and I believe that it was this encounter that gave him the inspiration for what, decades later, was to become that wonderful classic, *Bartleby & Co.*

There is a passage in *Bartleby* in which I'm convinced that Vila-Matas, without actually naming him, talks about Bevilacqua. You're so well read, I'm sure you know it by heart: "In the literature of No, there are certain works which not only are unwritten, but of which we know nothing, neither the subject, nor the title, the length or the style. We are told that such and such a person, a writer, is a well-known author. But of what? He denies his own paternity without even, like his famous ancestor, allocating himself the role of stepfather. Señor X claims not to be a writer, not to have written; vox populi contradicts him and asserts that his work, not read by anyone, is *remarquable*."

When Vila-Matas found out about Bevilacqua's death, he wrote to me, suggesting that the crime had intellectual roots. "What better solution for a pseudo-Bartleby, for the author of an evasive[1] book, than to make himself an evasive author. Now both of them, author and work, share the same empty shelf."

"Empty" may not be the best word to describe Bevilacqua at that time. Apprehensive, awkward, listless, yes, suspicious and distrustful, I would have to agree. That fear he had learnt during his last years

---

1. Or perhaps "evanescent" – I'm not sure how to read this word. Vila-Matas had (and still has) terrible handwriting.

in Argentina, which caused him to jump out of his skin every five minutes, to mistrust kindness, to keep secrets and opinions to himself, did not entirely disappear when he arrived in Spain.

An example. Soon after his arrival, Bevilacqua was taken by Andrea to one of those cafés on the Paseo Castellana that serve bad coffee at an exorbitant price, a favourite meeting place for the flocks of newly arrived South Americans. Tito Gorostiza, may he rest in peace, was ferreting around in that bag he always carried with him, a memento from Mendoza, searching for some quote he wanted to read to the others. Among the books he stacked up on the table was an anthology of stories published in Havana. When he saw it, Bevilacqua glanced over his shoulder, then picked up his jacket and quickly covered the book with it. He had gone quite pale. It took me a moment to understand why.

I don't think Bevilacqua regretted his exile in Madrid. On the contrary – he was enchanted by all that he *imagined* Spain to be. His good fortune in falling under the protection of Quita and Andrea meant that, rather than braving some downtown hostel, he had, from day one, been able to lodge in a flat in the Prospe area, not far from the Martín Fierro. There were already five other Argentine exiles living in the flat, among them Cornelio Berens, dubbed the "Flying Dutchman" because of his swift passage through so many countries.

Bevilacqua's room in the flat was small but full of light. Quita gave him a little money and Andrea – who was well acquainted with Latino survival methods – suggested that he go with one of the others to sell craftwork on the Calle Goya. You wouldn't believe how many famous names started off laying out their wares on that pavement! I have a dried-bean bracelet made by a gentleman who tops the best-seller list in his country now, Terradillos. Anyway, it was on the wide pavement of the Calle Goya that the Spanish chapter of Alejandro Bevilacqua's life began.

But Terradillos, forgive me, I'm getting ahead of myself: I see now that we had not quite finished the Argentine chapter. Let's go back for a moment, if you don't mind.

After he finished school, Bevilacqua had opted not to go to university, rejecting it as too systematic and authoritarian. At first, despite rumblings of protest from Señora Bevilacqua, he tried to make a living as a puppeteer. Later he found that he could make a little money by writing the text for those fotonovelas I mentioned earlier.

He came to this almost by accident, on one par-ticularly uneventful day, by imagining a script which told the unhappy, romantic tale (it would be an act of exorcism for him) of his love for Loredana. If you think about it, the subject lends itself to theatre: there's the infatuated adolescent, the indifferent beauty, the paternal and ineffectual old man, the hot pursuit through mountains and valleys, and the final disillusionment. He showed his script to Babar, who was working as a journalist on a financial newspaper and, far from pouring scorn on the idea, Babar suggested he send it to Editorial Jotagé, which specialized in soft pornography, sentimental magazines and fotonovelas. Thus began the literary career of Alejandro Bevilacqua. So much for that proverb, "The eagle doesn't catch flies".

Meanwhile, his grandmother, now old and frail, was increasingly prone to mental confusion and unreliable memories. Less intransigent, less determined, Señora Bevilacqua had become preoccupied and distracted. Little things slipped her mind: she forgot to order more olives or to check on the quality of the cold cuts. She made mistakes in the accounts, or left the kettle to boil dry on the stove. Once, Alejandro found her sitting in the kitchen, as though sleeping with her eyes open, black smoke swirling around her as a beef *matambre* burned to a crisp in the oven. Another time, Señora Bevilacqua rose before dawn, dressed in her Sunday best and woke up her grandson to tell him that she was going to the cemetery, "because they're waiting for me there". Alejandro felt obliged to spend more and more time with her, and watched her deteriorate day by day: her skin became transparent, her posture more stooped, her voice weaker; her gaze was unsteady, her hands shook.

One afternoon, on his way home after handing in a script and without knowing precisely why, Bevilacqua went a few stops farther than usual on the bus. It was dark by the time he had walked back and, at home, he found the door to the street ajar. He went upstairs without putting on the light. The scent of eucalyptus and of something else, both sweet and rancid, held him at the doorway to his grandmother's room. He heard a hoarse noise. In her bed, watched over by the orchestra of bewigged monkeys, the old lady's body had shrunk to the size of a puppet. Her curls fanned out extravagantly on the pillow, while everything else about her seemed almost impossibly small. Her pencilled eyebrows and pale lips heightened the sense of unreality, of something suspended at the point of undoing. Her grandson called her: the eyes opened, closed and opened once more. Looking at her, he felt those eyes were accusing him. It was the last time, he told me, that Señora Bevilacqua's reproving gaze fell on her grandson.

Her breathing became laboured, measured in long, calculated pauses. After a time, it ceased. Bevilacqua remembered that his grandmother would have wanted the last rites. But where to turn for this? Who would he find at this time of night? Where was the closest church? Eventually, he went to bed. The following morning, he called the undertakers.

A week after the funeral, during the long, inevitable requiem mass attended by La Bergamota's longest-standing clients, Bevilacqua reflected on his formidable grandmother's life. What remained of all this for him? What would become of him, orphaned and insecure? He was almost thirty, with no family and very few friends (loyal Babar could still be counted on, and some of the photographers from Jotagé). The time had come to define himself, to acquire a set of characteristics and a presence that were entirely his, with no residue of that rigorous woman who had wanted to consign her grandson to a life of cold cuts. He began with a gesture: when the priest came towards him holding out the communion wafer, Bevilacqua made some slight motion of rejection, and the priest was obliged to move on to the next communicant. Señora Bevilacqua was buried in the Chacarita cemetery. After the ceremony, Bevilacqua never returned to her grave.

And so on to 1967. Bevilacqua had just turned twenty-nine. He had inherited, without too much paperwork, his grandmother's house and the premises of La Bergamota, along with a respectable nest egg. To cut a long story short, he sold the properties, put the money in the bank and, by the time he was thirty, without asking himself why, he had embarked on a degree at the Faculty of Philosophy and Arts. That was where he met Graciela.

As you will have realized by now, a number of women were important in Bevilacqua's brief life. I told you that his adolescence was played out between the magnetic poles of two of them – the cold and austral grandmother and the northern, misty-eyed Loredana. In the second part of his life there were two others, equally opposed. But we shall come to them later.

Allow me an aside. It's strange how the dramas in our lives play out, over the years, with a small cast which, scene after scene, takes on all the characters. These are always the same: the hero or heroine, the older man, the ingenue, the mother figure, the villain, the loyal friend. In Bevilacqua's case, there were always two female performers: the strong, reserved woman, whom Bevilacqua obeyed while yearning to escape her clutches; the other an unattainable object of desire, capable of wounding him without even a glance in his direction. As for the men in his life, I can see at least a couple: first, the constant friend, as exemplified by Babar, who spoke little but was always there, serving as a bridge to the practical world; second, the educator, the guru, father confessor such as Don Spengler, whose role, to my chagrin, I ended up inheriting.

There is also a third one, now that I come to think of it: the invisible enemy.

But let's return to Graciela for a moment. She was a little younger than him, dark, slight, aggressive and intelligent. The first time they ever spoke was in a café opposite his faculty, where Bevilacqua had gone to do some revision for an exam and she was meeting with a group of protesters. I imagine that both of them felt rather old among so many adolescents. Bevilacqua had looked up from his page only to find himself gazing at Graciela's cleavage.

"Hey, you," he suddenly heard.

He realized that these words were directed at him and, taken aback, he said, "Me?"

"Yes, you. You staring at my tits?"

Bevilacqua buried his head in his book. When he finally looked up, Graciela had gone. Later they ran into each other in the same class. Inevitably, it was she who made the first move. She wanted to know what he did, what course he was studying, what his political beliefs were. Bevilacqua offered up one or two opinions. Graciela scoffed at them and recommended others. That first exchange set a pattern that varied very little during the many years of their relationship.

Graciela was the younger daughter of a couple of notaries. I think they were Armenians or something – at any rate, their surname was Arraiguran. They lived in Almagro, which says it all. Graciela did not want to be a writer, did not read literary magazines or care about the new French novel. She envisioned her future in some vaguely political post, but her natural vocation, for law, struck her as too close to her parents'. She thought that studying in the Faculty of Arts would give her a useful grounding in history and rhetoric. She was, apparently, an excellent speaker.

Look, Terradillos, I think that Graciela took Bevilacqua under her wing less to protect him than for the sake of having something to protect. People who saw them together said they made an ideal couple, but the more astute observers noticed how she had got her claws into him. Bevilacqua was alone in the world; he knew nothing of life's dangers; he lacked experience of human wiles. Graciela prided herself on being an expert in all that. She was amused by Bevilacqua's bewilderment, as one might be amused to see a moth lunging at a pane of glass it cannot see. I would say that she even married him to watch him crash into the glass.

They married, they bought a flat in Boedo, they finished their studies and got jobs – he as a teacher in a local school, she as an assistant in some faculty department or other. I know what you're thinking: how banal! Maybe, but, when one takes a backward look at history, every decision, every move, each step contributes to the gran finale, complete with drums, glockenspiel and cymbals.

Apparently Graciela began to organize meetings after class, at the university itself. Some union leader, a fellow traveller, a couple of Uruguayan intellectuals, a befuddled provincial writer – these became the founding members of a group predictably named Spartacus. She started coming home late at night, while Bevilacqua went to bed alone, leaving for her, on the kitchen table, half a portion of steak and chips bought at the corner café. During the long summer break, if Bevilacqua proposed a week or two in one of the quieter seaside resorts near Mar del Plata, Graciela would claim that she had to stay in the capital on some union business, and Bevilacqua would take off with a couple of detective novels to Necochea, Los Pinitos or Miramar without bearing any grudge.

One of those summers, he came home a day earlier than expected and found Graciela in a nightgown, making *café con leche* for one of her Uruguayan stalwarts. Nobody batted an eyelid, and Bevilacqua simply sat down at the table so that Graciela could serve him too. After that, Graciela's late nights became increasingly frequent. Sometimes Bevilacqua would not see her for a couple of days, then would return from work to find her in bed at six o'clock in the evening, fast asleep.

Bevilacqua had what I would call a "cohesive" vision of reality. By that I mean that he could take a multitude of disparate elements and partial facts and build from them a coherent and plausible scenario, complete with main and minor characters, intrigue and denouement. From the clues that Graciela was planning to leave him (the Uruguayan's breakfast was, I believe, the most compelling), Bevilacqua began to build up a picture of his wife's escapades in all their potentially scabrous detail. Sometimes he imagined her lover as an old trade-unionist, with a beer belly and moustache; at other times, as a youth who had barely started shaving. Once it was a leftist priest whose biceps bulged beneath his cassock, and another time a lecturer in law, slicked back and recalcitrant. One of the most persistent ghosts was a certain anonymous writer from Río Gallegos or Rawson, whose book of verse (I'm afraid it was called *Red March*) he found on Graciela's bedside table one day. "But I only love you," she told him. And Bevilacqua believed her.

One morning he decided to follow her. Graciela had told him that she was going on a demonstration, in the centre of town, close to the Obelisk. She was going to set off early in order to meet first with a delegation from the Caribbean – "brothers from the other Americas," she said, apparently, having been infected by that political argot which taints even the best intentions. The demonstration was due to start at noon. When Bevilacqua arrived, he noticed a small group forming outside the windows of the Casa Gold jewellers. He had thought that he would never find her in what he had imagined would be an enormous throng, like those shown on television. In fact he immediately spotted her, among some twenty or thirty people, helping two youths to lift up a banner. A little old man in a beret came over and shook his hand.

"Thanks for your support, *compañero*," said the old man.

"I'm with her," answered Bevilacqua, evasively.

"With Graciela?" laughed the old man. "God help you!"

They waited a bit, hoping to see their ranks swell, but no one else came. Then Graciela gave the order to advance.

Bevilacqua felt intensely uncomfortable, marching with the others along Diagonal, while from the pavements pedestrians paused to watch them and to shout out crude remarks or words of encouragement. Bevilacqua tried to keep his eyes fixed on Graciela, who was now at the head of the marchers, leading them in some pointless chant. When they arrived at the Town Hall, a battalion of mounted police emerged from a side street, blocking their way. The group came to a halt, but Graciela strode on. For a moment she alone confronted the horsemen; straight away the others followed her.

Bevilacqua did not feel afraid. This was his first demonstration, the first time he had ever been a part of something greater than himself, mingling with others, singing with them, moving with them. He was doing what the group did, without having to answer to anyone, without having to feel any responsibility for his actions. And he felt happy, anonymous and free – do you understand? For he had been chosen by the woman who was leading them all, his Graciela.

The first blow came simply as noise, with no immediate source or explanation. There followed a confusion of flying batons, kicks, shouting and neighing, a police car's siren. He saw the banner fall, the vast flank of a horse, a hand covered in blood. He heard a distant cry and felt a shooting pain in his ear. He saw Graciela slip away between two mounted police officers, and followed her.

All at once, someone grabbed him by the arm and dragged him towards a café. He let himself be dragged. Graciela made him sit down, then pressed a clutch of paper napkins to his left ear. When the waiter approached with an expression of concern, she calmly asked for two coffees and a glass of water. The waiter brought their order, and Graciela thrust another handful of napkins into the glass.

"This isn't a hospital," the waiter said.

"Up yours!" answered Graciela, "and bring the gentleman another glass of water." She drank her coffee in one gulp and slapped some money on the table.

"Congratulations," she said to Bevilacqua. "Not bad for a first time."

And with that she stood up and left. Bevilacqua never saw her again.

It strikes me now that there is something sketchy about Bevilacqua's life. In literary terms it amounts to nothing more than a collections of fragments, snippets and unfinished episodes. Any one of them could serve as the start of a great novel, one thousand pages long, profound and ambitious. My version of his life is closer to the style of the man himself: indecisive, undefined, inept. As I warned you at the start: I'm not the person best suited to tell you about him.

But a promise is a promise. After Graciela's disappearance, Bevilacqua lived alone in the flat in Boedo, teaching during the day and writing scripts at night. He saw Babar from time to time, and both realized that they no longer had anything in common. The last time they ran into each other in the street, neither of them even said hello, but walked on without stopping.

One afternoon, Bevilacqua bumped into one of the Uruguayans at the corner café, and they had no choice but to share a table. They struck up a half-hearted conversation about football, about the price of a cup of coffee, and then – under the guise of discussing a sick friend – about the vague rumours concerning what had happened to Graciela after the demonstration.

"Doctors have a hand in everything. You can't even die in peace."

"It's the nurses you can't trust. People who say they're going to give you an aspirin, then stick a scalpel in your back."

"Do you know the nurse in question?" asked Bevilacqua. "Are you sure there was one?"

"I'm not sure of anything, brother. Except of the grave, and even then I don't know if it will be in earth or water. But yes, there was one."

They parted without shaking hands, eyes cast down. In those days, you walked around Buenos Aires with your head bowed, trying neither to see nor hear, not saying anything. Above all, you tried not to think, because you began to believe that others could read your thoughts. (Later, in Madrid, Bevilacqua would discover that he could indeed think, but in the midst of such an overwhelming silence that he felt as though he were speaking on the moon, where the lack of air transmits no sound.)

Without Graciela, the passing of days seemed crushingly slow, with no progress or change. Everything seemed to happen at a remove. Bevilacqua realized now that she, with her rather brutal manner, her uninhibited sensuality, her many infidelities, had been behind all his actions, all his words. I'm not exaggerating. I'm simply telling you what I was able to glean from him. Graciela was his centre. Without her everything crumbled. He lost interest in the world. He stopped caring.

One morning, at dawn, he was picked up from the street by two silent men. Inside the car, which was taking him to prison, there were stickers on the doors, threatening anyone who tried to open them. They emptied his pockets while an enormous, asthmatic woman noted down every object – watch, pen, handkerchief, wallet – in an exercise book. After that they left him for hours in a windowless cell. It was a few days later that the sessions began. I'll spare you the details.

I don't want to describe the horrors that followed – and not because I am ignorant of them. Bevilacqua told me everything, or everything that can be told – which, in these cases, is not very much. Beneath the surface of all that we are able to put into words, lies that profound and obscure mass of the unspeakable, an ocean without light, swimming with blind, un-imaginable creatures. It was a world I glimpsed only fleetingly during our many meetings, charting the course of his extremely sad story. Because Bevilacqua's account skipped chapters, beginning at the end and then jumping back to the prologue. He started his story in Paradise, continued into the Inferno and finished up in Purgatory. And when he arrived there neither I, nor Andrea, Quita or any of the others who later claimed to have been loyal friends were a Virgil for him. Feel free to condemn me for it.

It must have been nearly a year after his arrival in Madrid when Bevilacqua rang the bell of my apartment, as he used to do two or three times a week. It was late. I had promised to hand in an article the next day (at the time I was writing for a French magazine that paid more than the stingy Spanish ones), and I had thus far written only one or two paragraphs. He didn't give me a chance to say anything. With an even more sorrowful expression than usual, he came in, sat on the only comfortable armchair and told me what had happened.

He said that, even from a distance, in the weary half-light of a winter afternoon in Madrid, he had known it was her. I assumed that he meant Graciela, but the woman he began to describe to me was quite different: a tiny body on top of extraordinarily long legs and a ridiculous hat that looked like a disproportionately large beak. Bevilacqua said that, in Buenos Aires, they had called her La Pájara, the Painted Bird, after that Spanish rhyme which you may know:

> The Painted Bird
> Sat on the green lemon tree.
> With its beak it cut the bough,
> With its beak it cut the bloom.

Bevilacqua had met her during his stint in prison, when she had come, wearing the very same hat, to visit one of his cellmates, Marcelino "El Chancho" – "The Pig" – Olivares. I expect you're wondering how, in one of those terrible prisons, anyone was allowed special privileges. I'll tell you how: local custom. *Primus inter pares* translates in my country as "There'll always be a favourite". El Chancho was one such. He was a Cuban exile who had arrived in Argentina at the end of the 1950s, before Fidel's Revolution. This curious hybrid of intellectual and businessman had managed to persuade various members of the military to let him invest their savings in Switzerland. He did make the investments – no one questions that – but it seems that as the tray was passing, he helped himself to a few titbits.

Unfortunately, the military men found him out and swore revenge; they went looking for him one dark night, and El Chancho was invited to change address. Let it never be said that the army doesn't reward services rendered, however, because even in prison El Chanco enjoyed certain privileges: visits from La Pájara, books, biscuits, cigarettes...

How this animal ended up in the same cell as our Bevilacqua, I shall never know. The sick methodology of those times defies comprehension, I'm sure you'll agree, Terradillos. Because Bevilacqua wasn't given to explanations. He never even showed any emotion when he was telling me these things. Doubtless there were dark currents flowing beneath the surface, but I swear that the impression given to a disinterested listener such as myself was of a tranquil lake into which one yearns to lob a stone, to cause a ripple or some sort of movement... I asked him why it was so strange to run into a woman he had known years before in Buenos Aires, in Madrid.

"Not strange, impossible," he answered. "La Pájara is dead. They killed her a few weeks before they let me out. I was in the cell when they came to break the news to El Chancho. We were blindfolded. But I remember it because one of the men went up to him and said, "Sincere condolences.""

The significance of Bevilacqua's words still eluded me. I told him, in what I hoped was a conclusive tone, that he simply couldn't be sure of having seen her, at that distance and in that poor light.

Bevilacqua took my arm: "Brother," he said, "she followed me."

I resigned myself to hearing him out.

Apparently, Bevilacqua had gone out for a walk around Plaza de Oriente, which in those days was quite a bit shabbier than it is now. It was cold. A chill wind whistled around the bushes, clustering dirty papers around their roots. The occasional hooded figure (I swear that you could still see black capes in Madrid at that time) passed by, hugging the walls of buildings. Bevilacqua suddenly caught sight of her across the square, close by the Campo del Moro. For a long time he stared at her in horror. Then began a game of cat and mouse.

Bevilacqua tried to lose her by running into the alleys around the Church of San Nicolás. On the other side of the Calle Mayor, he crossed various little squares leading to the San Miguel market, negotiating dead ends and hurrying down porticoes. Perhaps because of the weather, the time of the day, or the fact that it was a religious holiday – or perhaps Bevilacqua imagined all this later – it seemed as if everything were closed: shops, cafés, offices. All he could hear was the wind, and La Pájara's heels on the cobblestones. Bevilacqua no longer registered the names of the streets through which he was fleeing. He seemed to cross the same square several times, retracing his steps, going up a hill he was sure he had come down a few minutes earlier. The same scene kept repeating itself in monochrome: the black stones, the ashen fog, the marble-coloured lamp-posts. This flight of his seemed to be taking place in the past, as though, rather than running through spaces, he were running back through time. And every time he turned around, there it was, defined against the dusky light, her ever-present, ornithological silhouette. Finally he emerged into the Plaza de las Cortes and, recognizing the columns and steps, realized that he was close to my house.

I say "my house" because that is what I called it
when I lived there, but now that building – with its
balconies and long windows, with the imposing front
door which, in those days, relied on the services of
a nightwatchman, with its pavement forever stained
by Bevilacqua's blood – I think of as belonging to
him. If I were superstitious, I would call it a case of
satanic possession, of the kind you find in medieval
chronicles, because that place, which was mine for
such a long time, is inhabited now by the memory of
his languid, melancholic, persistent figure. I think I
even intuited, during his perorations, this inevitable
outcome: that Bevilacqua would eventually take over
everything that was mine.

Anyway, I managed to calm him down. I said
that he should return to Andrea's flat and not worry
her with his fantastical stories. "These things," I
said, more out of weariness than conviction, "sort
themselves out after a good rest." I was generous
enough to suggest he seek consolation in the arms
of that young girl.

Because, you see, Bevilacqua had taken Andrea
too. Andrea, Quita's right hand, must have been
about twenty-five then. Her mother, a reader of
Spanish literature, had named her after the heroine
of Carmen Laforet's *Nada* and, in Andrea, there
was certainly something of that novel's rebellious

and sensual protagonist. Andrea herself was more into the literature of the New World, and when we first met I don't know if it was my appearance or my passport that seduced her.

Andrea was rather small, with straight, short hair and something of an angora rabbit about her. Her Arabic eyes looked out behind blue-framed spectacles. At that time my sexuality was more eclectic than nowadays: youth is willing to try anything. I confess that I fell in love with her immediately, as one is attracted to an anonymous traveller on an escalator – a face picked at random among those in the opposite line.

My friend: I've already told you that I met Bevilacqua some time after moving to Madrid. Andrea and I must have been going out for a couple of months by then. I was not much older than her; Bevilacqua, as I mentioned before, was ten years older than me. He was elegant and slender; I've always been a bit flabby and scruffy. Age and poise won out. Andrea must have felt that Bevilacqua was endowed with more prestige and a better lineage. It's true that, along with the habitual expression of a slaughtered ram, a swatch of grey hairs lent him an aristocratic look, giving him the appearance of one of those characters that girls of Andrea's age (if they like Latin American literature) lap up from the likes of

Bioy Casares or Carlos Fuentes. On top of her desk, which was tastelessly adorned with little tropical plants and toy animals, I once discovered a framed photograph of a twenty-something Bevilacqua, in a French beret, arms crossed and looking like a prophet who's expecting God knows what. In the face of such competition, I beat an honourable retreat. I believe that Bevilacqua never fully knew how generously I had yielded him my place.

Andrea began by introducing Bevilacqua into the small artistic circles which were starting to flourish in Madrid, in dark, smoky basements that hoped to imitate, after a fashion, the *vie bohème* of Saint-Germain-des-Près some twenty years earlier. She introduced Bevilacqua to a way of dressing that would set him apart from the lugubrious masses and, given his horror of clothes shops, she started buying him tweed jackets and silk bow ties. Finally, she decided that Bevilacqua should move in with her. More or less forcibly, she took his few belongings to her flat in the Chueca district and even offered to pay the Flying Dutchman any outstanding rent. Andrea divided her wardrobe in two, offering the more spacious part to Bevilacqua (even though she had ten times as many clothes) and, in a corner of the room, she set up a little table so that he would have somewhere comfortable to string his coloured-bean necklaces. Next to the tool box, she discreetly placed a reading lamp, a ream of paper and a portable Olivetti.

Since the first time Bevilacqua had been introduced to her, Andrea had resolved that this writer (never mind that he was a writer of fotonovelas) should take up his pen again. That was her mission: to rescue her beloved genius from a Bartleby-style indolence. Andrea believed fervently in the magnificent, re-sounding work that Bevilacqua, terrified of revealing it to the world, must surely be carrying in the depth of his soul. Andrea would be his midwife, his keeper, his tutor.

Vila-Matas assures me that, in the case of non-writing writers, someone usually pops up who refuses to accept this creative silence and tries to provoke an outburst of all that has not been expressed. Rather than admit that the writer exists precisely because of what he does *not* produce, this person sees in the absence of work a promise of great things to come. Andrea's relationship with Bevilacqua confirms the master's thesis.

Months passed, however, and Bevilacqua did not write. He spent every night stringing beans. Every morning he set off for Calle Goya, where he spread out his mat. Some afternoons he spent in bored resignation with Andrea at a poetry reading or a private view. But, to Andrea's great concern, the ream of paper remained intact and the Olivetti unopened.

One day, when Bevilacqua had gone off to sell his knick-knacks, Andrea decided to clean up the flat and, on removing a pile of suitcases and boxes from the wardrobe, she spotted the old Pluna bag that Bevilacqua had brought over from Buenos Aires, a shirtsleeve protruding from it. Thinking that Bevilacqua must have forgotten some item of clothing that needed washing, Andrea emptied the bag and found, at the bottom of it, a rectangular packet, wrapped in plastic. She opened it. It was a bundle of handwritten papers, the first of which bore a title: *In Praise of Lying*. There was no name, either on the title page or the end page.

As you can imagine, Andrea began to read, and devoured the manuscript in one sitting. As she finished, the bells of Santa Bárbara were striking six o'clock in the evening. Andrea quickly bundled everything else back into the wardrobe and set off for the Martín Fierro, taking the novel with her. There she placed it in a drawer of her desk and locked it. (I remember that desk, that drawer and that key so well!)

Although Andrea worked out the details of her plan little by little, the main thrust of it had come to her immediately, when she had barely read the first paragraphs. Bevilacqua was a writer, as she had always suspected. Not of fotonovelas and other pap. He was a real writer, the author of a work of art. Because *In Praise of Lying* was (and is, as you who have read it will know) a great novel.

I know you're thinking about that handful of bad reviews which, unsurprisingly, sought to redress the balance. I also read some sceptical and bad-tempered articles by a handful of cynical critics, including Pere Gimferrer in Barcelona and Noé Jitrik from his Mexican exile. I read them, and they honestly did not alter, in the slightest, my first opinion. Nor did they change Andrea's – which, believe me, is not to be sniffed at. Because Andrea knew good literature when she saw it. She took pleasure, I admit, in minor works, those well-written and perfectly agreeable novels that make a journey shorter or while away the night hours. But a work of genius is something else, as Andrea knew all too well. And the one she had just read was part of that select, literary Olympus: it belonged on that shelf which Andrea reserved only for books without which, as someone once said, "the world would be poorer". *In Praise of Lying* must not be hidden away. Nobody had the right to deprive the world of something so beautiful. Andrea (for all her small size, that woman was a *force de la nature*, as you might say, Terradillos) would be its herald, its standard-bearer. She would see it published to a fanfare. She would distribute it by hand, if necessary, to ensure that it reached the few luminaries who were beginning to appear on Spain's dismal intellectual firmament. And not just Spain's; Bevilacqua was going to be read in the remotest corners of the globe. Andrea felt herself possessed by a kind of evangelizing fever. If she had come to me for advice at that time, I would have cautioned prudence, reflection. But she didn't. She went to Camilo Urquieta, instead.

I keep forgetting that you don't know any of these people! Being so young (forgive me, Terradillos, but, at my age anyone with less than half a century under his belt is a stripling) you don't know any of these names, which were so famous in their day. Urquieta was (he died a long time ago, poor old thing) your typical born editor. Some people embody their *métier*: they are a hundred per cent carpenters, guitar-players and bankers to the core, and can never be anything else – they were that thing in their mothers' womb and they will continue to be it after their last breath, as scattered dust, you might say, as part of the air we breathe. Every day, my friend, we inhale the ashes of military men, podiatrists, prostitutes and, why not, those editorial ashes of Camilo Urquieta.

Let me tell you about him. Urquieta was born in Cartagena, in Murcia – something he always brought up when dealing with Murcian authors. Early on, he moved to Madrid. He was first there under Franco, then during the decades of slow change. Later, by representing the writers of the emerging cultural scene – the *Movida* – he managed to find himself a spot in the world of letters. He was an early editor of Hugo Wast and Chardin, later of a short life of St Thomas and etiquette manuals, such as *The Polite Child* and *Good Manners*; then, from a cautious *Introduction to Theosophy*, translated by Zenobia Camprubí, he suddenly went on to publish the works of several young Latin American writers who were taking their first steps in the world of books. Courting notoriety with an anthology of vaguely erotic literature, he demonstrated once and for all that nothing in this new Spain was as it had been before. Urquieta knew instinctively what to publish, at what time and in what manner and, above all, how to sell it and then start the whole process again. There are at least half a dozen publishing houses still running which began life under Urquieta. During the time we're talking about, Urquieta was running an imprint – the vigorously named Sulphur – that dared to include in its catalogue all those poets published in Argentina and Mexico which had previously only been available under the counter in certain dangerous shops. Ask Ana María Moix, who knows much more about that chapter of Spanish publishing than I do.

Andrea knew Urquieta because, in the small social circle of those days, it was impossible not to know him. And he, predictably flattered that a beautiful and intelligent girl like Andrea would ask his advice, offered it to her in a dingy café next to Angel Sierra's wine bar. Urquieta frequented this place, apparently, because one of his poets – Cornelio Berens, I believe – had described it in a Nerudian ode as "a mussel bravely clinging / to the prow of an old battleship". Others says that Urquieta stayed out of the editorial offices because of the uncomfortable possibility of running into a debt collector there.

At the back of this café, Urquieta had a table reserved for life. To reach it (I, too, have made the pilgrimage!) one had to go down a series of invisible steps, then grope one's way along a corridor crammed with chairs and tables. One mean candle ("it creates atmosphere," claimed the café's owner, who was from Salamanca) grudgingly illuminated the editor's face, which was smooth and creamy, like the paper in a deluxe edition. Urquieta, I don't know if I've told you, had no body hair, and wore a rather unconvincing wig. But nothing could disguise his lack of eyebrows and eyelashes and, in the gloom, one had the disagreeable impression of sitting opposite someone not entirely human.

Of course I don't know what they said to one another, but I can imagine (humour me here) the anxious, ardent questions of little Andrea, *toute feu, toute flamme*, as you French say, and the solemn, know-it-all answers of Urquieta, playing part Père Goriot, part Casanova. Andrea must have explained to him about her discovery, the need to publish what she regarded as a prodigious work, the need to conceal from its author the fate of his book. Urquieta, smitten but cautious, must have asked for time to look at it and give her his opinion.

You already know the rest of the story. Urquieta's decision to publish *In Praise of Lying*. The rumours that began to circulate around the secret future bestseller. The race to be one of the first to read it. The scandal of the galley proofs. Suspicions around the name of the secret author. The invariably over-conservative sales forecasts. Even though it was December and people were focused on Christmas shopping, all Madrid seemed to be absorbed by one topic.

Finally, the long-awaited evening came. At about seven o'clock, a small but select group began to gather in the cramped, over-heated space of the Antonio Machado cultural centre. They certainly numbered more than the visitors who usually attended such presentations, which were rare at the time. I had received my invitation the day before. At first, I thought I might not go, because that same evening I was returning to Poitiers for a couple of days to attend a seminar, and the prospect didn't thrill me. I mean to say, what would life be without that constant flow of vexatious obligations, of insipid engagements, of frustrated desires!

Terradillos, let me set the scene: the guest of honour nowhere to be seen. Andrea, at the door, anxiously looking out for him. Two or three journalists waiting impatiently. Berens making jokes about the well-known modesty of celebrities. Quita wrapped in her fur stole, annoyed as hell, asking Tito Gorostiza if he really did not know what had happened to our Alejandro. Gorostiza sulking.

Finally Urquieta made an announcement saying that they could wait no longer.

The proceedings were opened by a certain actress, a rising star in Spanish cinema, who read a few pages from the novel. The audience, doubtful at first, listened with increasing delight, bursting into applause at the end. After that Urquieta spoke. As you'd expect, he made an allusion to the new voices emerging from the New World, to the linguistic debt repaid now by the River Plate to the cradle of Cervantes, to that inspiration born on the legendary pampas between Eldorado and Tierra del Fuego. He concluded by citing various names from the Sulphur backlist who (so he claimed) were already classic authors. More applause. Then Bevilacqua appeared.

Borne along on Andrea's arm, he seemed to be dragged to the platform rather than guided there. Urquieta shook his hand, half-turning so that the photographer could get a shot of them together. Then, with a kind of reverence, he stepped aside to let him speak. Bevilacqua stared at the microphone as though it were some strange creature, blinked and raised his gaze to the back of the room; he looked around for Andrea and, finding her behind him, looked ahead again. With difficulty, he lit a cigarette.

There is nothing longer than a public silence; this one of Bevilacqua's must have lasted at the very least five endless minutes. We waited, perplexed, feeling uneasy for him more than for ourselves. Suddenly, as though something had hit him in the face, he looked down, got down from the platform, forged a path through the crowd and made a swift escape through the front door. I say "escape", because that was the impression he gave us. Of an animal in flight.

With a few, halting words, Urquieta brought the proceedings to a close. It was apparent that even he, a seasoned master of ceremonies, was baffled. Bevilacqua's behaviour was so strange, so inexplicable that everyone (myself included, of course) felt stunned and defrauded, as if the man who had run away was someone else. I went up to Andrea, to see if she could explain what had happened. The poor girl was on the brink of tears and, without answering me, tried to cover her face. Tito Gorostiza, always so gentlemanly, spoke consolingly to her, while pocketing two of the bottles of sherry that Urquieta had laid on (because a good businessman knows when to be generous) in preparation for the final toast. Berens, who doesn't miss a thing, joined us and, with those lizard features of his, launched into a rant.

"I suppose this is the avant-garde way of doing things, eh? Rudeness as a literary style. And there I was, thinking Spain was above the silly posturing we're used to in South America! Because you know what's going to happen now? This snub will be interpreted as a revolutionary manifesto – just wait and see. We come from a country where nobody is surprised to see artists getting mixed up in politics, "the lowest of all human activity" as one of my fellow countrymen describes it. But why shit all over the new nest? What's the point of that?"

"Berens, weren't you mixed up in politics yourself?" asked Paco Ordoñez, who had recently started working at the news agency EFE. "Isn't that why they arrested you?"

"You'll always find a clover / Amid the grass unseen / Which when you turn it over / Shines with a braver green. You can have that quotation free. I wrote it," Berens replied.

I'm not insensitive to the suffering of others. I saw that Andrea was still anxious. She clearly wanted to leave. Without saying goodbye to anyone, I took her arm and led her out into the street. She didn't put up much resistance. We found a café a few blocks away. When she had calmed down, I asked her what had happened. The poor thing said she didn't know, that Bevilacqua seemed suddenly to have taken fright, that it must have been her fault for not consulting him, that she had thought the publication would make him happy, that she had only done it for him, so that his genius would be recognized.

I told her that that would still be the case. I was in no doubt that *In Praise of Lying* was an important work.

"If you say so," she said, in a tone of voice which – given that I am easily moved – suddenly made her seem like a little girl. Isn't there something touching about the absolute faith of people in love? All these years later, it still makes me shiver to remember Andrea's voice.

I answered that of course I thought so, that this was my professional opinion. "Without a doubt," I assured her. "The critics will be on your side. And you know how harsh they usually are. But in this case they'll be kinder – I'm sure of it."

I paid, and we left. Freezing fog was making the bad driving conditions worse, and it was a stop-start journey to her house. After leaving her, I went home, in a pensive mood.

There he was. Bevilacqua was standing outside my front door, the tip of his cigarette glowing like lamplight in the fog. The nightwatchman was watching him charily. I seemed to be tasked with calming people's nerves that night. You know me, Terradillos. You know what I'm like. I was already that way in my youth. I tried to soothe them both.

We were scarcely through the door when Bevilacqua began to tell me everything. Andrea's discovery had upset him very much, and to see, all of a sudden, the printed book had plunged him into a nightmare in which he felt utterly powerless. I reminded him of Freud's discovery that nothing is accidental, that all events are prompted by something within us. But Bevilacqua was neither offended nor annoyed. He merely felt lost, stunned, incapable of expressing himself (he used an endless stream of words to make this point, of course). Up there on the

ALL MEN ARE LIARS

platform, before that avid audience, hemmed in on the right by Urquieta, who terrified him, and on the left by Andrea, whom he loved, but who also scared him, the poor man had not known what to do or say. Then he caught sight of them. Him and her. The two of them. Right there in the audience. Sitting with everyone else. Smiling. He with his horrible dark glasses. She with her little hat.

"Who?" I asked, pointlessly.

"El Chancho and La Pájara," he answered. "El Chancho Olivares and La Pájara Pinta."

"Not your zoological phantoms again, Bevilacqua," I said, to mollify him. "Wasn't La Pájara dead? Wasn't El Chancho, as you call him, in prison for conning a military man? They're hardly going to let him take a leave of absence!"

"I can't explain it," he said, "but they were there."

"All right," I said, hurriedly, because my train was leaving in a couple of hours. "Let's see. Suppose it was them. Suppose the grave could not hold her and prison bars were not enough for him. What does it matter to you? It's not as though they blame Alejandro Bevilacqua for their woes."

Bevilacqua shot me a look of terror, wringing his long yellow fingers as though he were washing them. "Brother," he entreated me. "You're about to go to France for a few days. Would you let me stay here, in your house, just for the weekend? I promise not to touch anything. I just don't have the courage to deal with the journalists, with Andrea, with Urquieta, with..." He let the sentence hang.

What can I say – I'm a bit soft-hearted, as you know. Someone asks me for something and I can't say no. Also, if I'm honest, I didn't like the idea of leaving the house unoccupied for more than a few hours. I'd heard of several robberies taking place in the neighbourhood, invariably when the occupiers were away. I had a hunch that the nightwatchman was passing on information, but of course it was impossible to prove this. And to be fair, Bevilacqua was a very tidy man. So I agreed. I swear that he embraced me with tears in my eyes; he would have kissed me if I'd let him. I picked up my suitcase, gave him a copy of my key and let him walk me to the door.

After I finished my Sunday seminar (the turn-out was disappointing; from December to March the French show little interest in anything), I took the train back to Madrid. The Ávila landscape was visible through my window as, yawning and with my *café con leche* slopping cheerfully onto its saucer, I opened a newspaper the waiter had brought and read the terrible news that Bevilacqua had died. It was Tuesday. The newspaper said that on Sunday morning an early riser had come across the body in a pool of congealed blood. A photograph showed the nightwatchman pointing an accusing finger at my balcony. The article gave no further details, but lingered instead on the irony of this fêted author having found fame such a short time before his tragic end. It quoted Urquieta, for whom the new literature had just lost one of its best voices. On the same page there was an ad in which the Sulphur publishing house reminded the public of the merits of *In Praise of Lying*. I reread the article several times. A death in one's immediate circle is particularly hard to take in.

When I got home, the nightwatchman advised me, with evident satisfaction, that the police wanted to question me. Not many people like the police. The Swiss, the English maybe. Not me. With a growing sense of unease, I started looking around this flat which no longer felt like mine. Violent acts render familiar things alien, and besides, in this case, there were traces of Bevilacqua in every room, on all the furniture. On the dining-room table were the remains of a frugal supper. On the sofa (and I usually keep everything so tidy) there was a waistcoat, several shirts and a towel. The bed was unmade. I swear that I felt I could never again sleep on that mattress, on that pillow, as if Bevilacqua had died there, between my sheets. After a while I went out onto the balcony, whose balustrade now struck me as dangerously low. For the first time in my life, I felt vertigo.

I resigned myself to the worst: discomfort, uncertainty, insomnia. I unpacked my suitcase, put Bevilacqua's things away in his (which sat in a corner of the room, like a loyal dog awaiting its master's return) and spent the rest of the day cleaning the flat from ceiling to floor with Ajax. I slept badly that night.

It must have been eight o'clock in the morning when the doorbell rang. Not finding my glasses on the bedside table, I groped my way towards the front door. I could just make out two hazy shapes. One, small and bald, belonged to the nightwatchman. The other introduced itself as Inspector Mendieta, from the Investigation Squad. Apologizing for the fact that I was still in pyjamas, I invited the inspector in, then closed the door in the nightwatchman's face.

You have good eyesight, Terradillos, and I bet you can't imagine how awkward it is to talk to someone whose features are a blur. My discomfort was exacerbated by the paradoxical character of Inspector Mendieta. Even without glasses, I could tell that he was both cordial and menacing, paunchy and moustachioed, like a Mexican Father Christmas.

He asked me to sit down as though we were in his house, not mine.

In a way I was almost disappointed that he didn't treat me more severely. He asked a few obvious questions (why Bevilacqua had been in my house, how long we had known each other, what his state of mind had been when I left him, if anything unusual had happened in the last days of his life), and he wondered if I would be staying in Madrid in the following weeks. Then he took a look around the flat, pausing for several minutes on the balcony without saying anything. He sat down again.

"The rail is very low, isn't it?" he suddenly said.

"Not just mine," I protested. "All the balconies are the same. It's part of the design. *Art nouveau*," I explained. My fuzzy vision was really annoying me and, when I noticed how bothered I was, it made me feel even more bothered. I began to talk about Madrid's *art nouveau*, comparing it to Barcelona's. Apparently not listening, Mendieta got to his feet and went back out to the balcony. I stopped talking. When we said goodbye, I felt accused, without knowing why.

I said before, Terradillos, that the death of someone close has something unreal about it. That's true, but there's a solidity and a substance to it as well. Those deaths that take place out there in the world, those hundreds of thousands of deaths that swamp us every day – they're insubstantial in their vast anonymity. That of a friend, on the other hand, wrenches from our very core something that belongs to us, and to which we belong. I think I've been clear on this point: I didn't love Bevilacqua. And yet, the fact that he had died there, in my house, under my momentarily absent nose, hurt like a pulled tooth, like a cut finger. Something was missing, now, from my life's routine, something regular, albeit a bit insipid, a bit boring and annoying: the tall, thin, pale and tormented shadow of Alejandro Bevilacqua.

The following weeks were difficult for me. I wrote a few articles for newspapers, continued to read dry research documents for my book, visited the welcoming reading room at the National Library – but in all these things I felt now like a man who's lost a limb or an eye. Unconsciously, I was always waiting for the door to open and for that very familiar voice to start recounting some tedious episode from his life.

Bevilacqua was buried in the Almudena cemetery, as inappropriate a choice as one can imagine: its ancient grandiosity didn't suit his character. Have you ever been there? It's all stone angels and broken urns, a phoney decadence standing in for the all-too-real decay of the flesh. "I have walked on the Andes" – that should have been his epitaph. But only his name and dates are there.

Of course it was Urquieta's decision that his final resting place should be the Almudena. Beneath a few conventional cypresses, the editor repeated (with some respectful modifications) the speech he had made at the book launch. Flesh remains, the word takes flight. If you were looking for an example on this earth of *sic transit*, Bevilacqua's funeral would have provided an unforgettable one.

Now that I think of it, the ceremony at the Almudena was like a grotesque parody of that other one, a few weeks earlier, at the Antonio Machado centre, a gloomy *da capo*, as unsettling as a shadow. The same people, the same words, but what had been happy excitement at the success of someone hitherto unknown was now replaced by the terrible sadness of his premature demise. I see them as clearly now as if I had photographed them. Berens and the other comrades from the flat in Prospe, faithful friends, standing beside a great broken urn; Quita and that young journalist, Ordóñez, on the threshold of a lugubrious mausoleum; my poor Andrea, as grief-stricken as one of those stone angels draped over the tombstones. The usual busybodies were there too, anonymous people drawn by the lure, the pleasure and perversity of someone else's grief. And among the unknown faces, a couple who looked vaguely familiar: he was short, rough-shaven, with dark glasses prominent beneath a black, broad-brimmed hat; she, tall with a big nose, sporting a green helmet, topped with a pheasant's feather. I asked Quita, who was talking to Ordóñez, if she knew them.

Only then did I realize that Quita had turned quite pale. I never would have guessed that Bevilacqua's death could affect her so greatly. She looked at me as though she didn't see me at all, distractedly searching among the tombs for the one person who was absent.

"They're Cuban," she said, finally, with a sigh. "Recent arrivals. He writes, she reads."

A light drizzle began to fall. "Nice literary touch," I thought to myself.

I saw Andrea walk away amid a procession of umbrellas. I hurried to catch up with her.

"If you need anything…" I began to say.

"If I do, I'll let you know," she answered with an abruptness I put down to her sorrow. I squeezed her shoulder and let her go on her way.

In the following weeks, I tried to see the Martín Fierro gang as little as possible. The time comes when these sorts of relationships – based to a degree on nostalgia and shared politics – draw to a close without us knowing how or why. Something in these exiled communities unravels or comes unstuck, people go their own way and, if I see you in the street,

I may not even stop. I knew that my time in Madrid was coming to an end.

I packed my suitcases, boxed up my books and paid my outstanding bills. I spent my last morning in the city walking, indulging my nostalgia. As I crossed Calle del Pinar, I heard someone call me. It was Ordóñez. I told him that I was returning to France. Ordóñez made some joking remark about the virtues of French cuisine. We said goodbye cordially, and then he remembered something that he wanted to tell me.

"Hey, Manguel. Those people in the cemetery you were asking Quita about. The Cubans. Apparently they're wanted by the police. I'm just telling you because you seemed interested."

Then I realized why those two had looked familiar, and I remembered that frightened description that Bevilacqua had given me. I began to understand that something, whether horrible or banal, which had bound the ghostly Argentinian to the fantastic Cuban, had come to an end now that one of them could no longer tell his version of events. It was another one of those stories that belong to the "archive of silence", as we refer to that infamous period in my country's history.

The encounter with Ordóñez depressed me even more. I wandered off through the streets of the

Prospe, with its ochre façades and broken paving stones. Almost without thinking, I arrived at the door of the Martín Fierro. I climbed the stairs. Quita was on her own, going through files at the reception desk, which had now been cleared of Andrea's things, of her little plants, her toys, her framed photograph of Bevilacqua. I was shocked to see how tired she looked, her bronzed skin tinged by a whitish lichen, a lock of grey hair falling over her forehead. Quita, who felt about grooming the same way Poles feel about Mass... We waffled on about this and that, and then I asked her to please come and visit me if she was ever passing through France. I dared not speak the name of our absent friend.

She was the one who mentioned it. I was almost at the door when Quita put a hand on my arm.

"Albertito, don't forget me," she said, with that despicable habit of shrinking her friends with diminutives. "Now that our Alejandrucho's no longer here... And Titito's gone..."

The ellipsis called for some words of consolation, but I had not been informed about Gorostiza's departure and so I didn't know what to say. I confess that the news hardly surprised me. I always considered the relationship between Quita and that uptight Argentinian to be a little unsavoury. Love affairs between patrons and their protégés never last.

Just think of poor Tchaikovsky with his widowed millionairess, Nadezhda von Meck.

I covered Quita's hand with my own, to console her, but Quita instantly whipped it away, as if scorched by my touch.

"Has an Inspector Mendieta come to see you?" she suddenly asked.

I said that he had.

"And what did you tell him?"

I made a brief summary of our somewhat uninspiring conversation.

"Did he ask you about me?"

"You?" I said, surprised. "No, of course not. We talked about balconies."

"You swear that you didn't say anything about me, or poor Tito, or anyone else?"

I swore that I didn't.

Then she told me something which I am going to tell you and which I must ask remain *entre nous*. I don't want to harm such an honourable woman needlessly. Quita was at my house the night that Bevilacqua died. It seems that his behaviour had alarmed her, as it had the rest of us. And you know what it's like with women who are a bit older: the slightest upset triggers their maternal instinct, and they feel they need to gather their chicks under their ample wings. Knowing that he was staying at my house (because in the literary world, everyone knows everything), Quita went to see him, to ask if there was anything she could do to help. The Bevilacqua who greeted her had grown even paler beneath his sallow skin, and his eyes, which were already naturally very dark, looked now (so said Quita) like hollows in a skull. Quita clutched him to her bosom, stroking his brow. But after a few minutes she began to feel that Bevilacqua wasn't happy to see her; in fact, he seemed to want her to leave, given that he hadn't even opened the door that led from the hall to the sitting room. Quita asked if any friends had come to see how he was. Bevilacqua said nothing. Well, I mean, what can you do? Quita may have the patience of a Griselda, but she has her self-respect too. She didn't push things. But before leaving, she thought she heard someone move behind the door leading from the hall. Of course, she thought that it was another woman and, with characteristic generosity, decided to leave the field clear. The last thing she ever said to Bevilacqua was that if he needed to speak to someone, he could always come to her.

"They were my last words," she repeated, "I swear."

I reassured her that nobody could have prevented what was about to happen, and that knowing that a woman like her cared about his fate must surely have been a great consolation to him, when the moment came to make his terrible decision.

On the train back to Poitiers, I started thinking about the sad story to which I had been an unwilling witness those last three months. Who was the man that I had known by the name of Alejandro Bevilacqua? Who had been that strange character who was at different times explicit and evasive, luminous and opaque? You're a writer, Terradillos (a journalist, I know, but that also counts), so you know how difficult it is to make the artist coincide imaginatively with his work. On one side is the literary creation, endlessly transformed through our readings and rereadings; on the other, the author, a human being with his own physical characteristics, his inherited delusions and weaknesses, his failings. Think of one-armed Cervantes, short-sighted Joyce, syphilitic Stendhal... you know what I mean.

But, just suppose we had never come to know of Bevilacqua? Suppose he had died an anonymous death in that military prison in Argentina? *In Praise of Lying* would still be considered a masterpiece, but in a different way, perhaps more perfect, more complete – at the risk of repeating myself. I mean: if it had no identified author, we would have read the novel like some lost text by a Latin Thomas Mann, an enlightened Unamuno, but with a sense of humour. We would have brought to his flow of words our own versions of that universe, our most subtle intuitions and our most secret experiences. Because, even if you know that that innocent, grey, rather doltish character was behind such a clever portrait of our times and its passions, *In Praise of Lying* is a book to which you can return time and time again. One reader will see the book as comedy, another as lyrical tragedy, a third as a ferocious political satire, a fourth as a melancholic elegy to a vanished past. There will even be (as I was telling you there were), readers who are blind to the work's genius, readers who, through lack of feeling or jealousy, are incapable of recognizing its unique mastery. In my opinion, *In Praise of Lying* succeeds in capturing the world that we knew (no mean feat) through the eyes of a perceptive and discreet witness capable of putting it into words, warts and all. It will be interesting to see if future readers one day speak of Unamuno as a philosophical incarnation of Bevilacqua, or of Thomas Mann as the Bevilacqua of Lübeck.

The characters from the drama have vanished now. Quita was consumed by cancer in the final days of last millennium. I never heard anything more from Andrea. As for Berens, who considered himself an immortal poet, nobody recites him now, least of all himself: he was committed some time ago to a psychiatric clinic in Santander. Gorostiza, as I discovered much later, chose his own fate. I don't know about the others.

Only one of them did not disappear altogether. From my house, here in France, I can still see a tall figure striding along the pavement of Calle del Prado. I see it stop at my door and climb the stairs to my apartment, I hear his hoarse voice greeting me, embarking on the familiar stories, while his eyes fix on mine and his fingers grip my arm to keep me from escaping or keeling over with boredom and fatigue. I can see him from here. And, Terradillos, even if, as I have often said, I am the least qualified person to talk about this character, there are days when I suddenly find myself, for no particular reason, thinking about him and his curious literary fate, or about the calumnies that were later heaped upon him, and about the wages of envy and sin.

And I say to myself, "Fancy that. You once knew Alejandro Bevilacqua."

2

MUCH ADO ABOUT NOTHING

> DON PEDRO: Officers, what offence have these men done?
>
> DOGBERRY: Marry, sir, they have committed false report, moreover they have spoken untruths, secondarily they are slanders, sixth and lastly they have belied a lady, thirdly they have verified unjust things, and to conclude they are lying knaves.
>
> William Shakespeare
> *Much Ado about Nothing*, v, 1

Alberto Manguel is an asshole. Whatever he told you about Alejandro, I'll bet my right arm it's wrong, Terradillos. Manguel is one of those types who see an orange and then swear it's an egg. "What, and *orange-coloured*?" you say. Yes. "And *round*?" Yes. "Does it smell of *blossom*?" Yes. "So, *like an orange*?" Yes, but it's definitely an egg. No, nothing is true for Manguel unless he's read it in a book. As for everything else, he'll concede only what he wants. The slightest insinuation, the smallest detail, sets him off on a wild-goose chase.

I'll tell you something, Terradillos – and you're not going to believe this: there was a time when he thought I had the hots for him. Can you imagine? Me? For Manguel! In those days the poor man was as indecisive as a swinging gate. During the weeks that he pursued me, he persuaded himself that I was interested in him, and all because I had asked him some stuff about an Argentinian writer I was reading. It was pathetic to see him traipsing round to the Martín Fierro, looking for me in the café, offering to walk me home – though less so for me, because I grew absolutely sick of him. Quita wiped the floor with him. Did you know she called him "Manganese" behind his back? "There's Manganese," she would say to me, "filling two chairs in the waiting room. See if you can shift him." But it was hopeless. Only after Alejandro and I moved in together did he stop following me around like a lapdog.

I don't know why Alejandro liked talking to him so much. You probably know more about such things, being a journalist. Alejandro talked about his life partly to relive it and partly to show off. Perhaps it amused him to entertain Manguel, the way it can be amusing to entertain a rather stupid dachshund. Or perhaps Alejandro went to see him precisely because Manguel didn't listen to what he was saying, but extrapolated outlandish literary stories from what he was hearing. Manguel would tell me something that he swore Alejandro had said to him, and I would just stare at him thinking – this fool, what planet's he on?

I think Manguel's inability to pay attention comes from too much reading. All that fantasy, all that invention – it has to end up softening a person's brain. I must have been barely twenty-five at that time, and Manguel was under thirty, but I felt a thousand times more experienced, more real than him. I used to listen to him and think to myself: at his age, and still playing with toy soldiers.

I bet Manguel painted you a picture of Alejandro as a man defeated and morose. Am I right? A victim finished off by years of suffering and persecution or whatever. Well it's true, of course, about the prison, and that can't have been a bundle of laughs. But apart from that, Alejandro was the opposite of a broken man. His setbacks galvanized him and made him stronger. Even as a boy.

I'm the one you should listen to, Terradillos. Because I'm from the land of your ancestors. Because Alejandro told me his whole life story in all its intimate, dirty details. You know, of course, that he was brought up by his grandmother, a woman who must have been tough, having to struggle alone throughout her life. I feel sorry for her, poor soul, because I also have some experience of these things. Alone and in charge of a crafty fox like Alejandro. She only had to look away for a moment and Alejandro would be going through her handbag, or nipping into the back room with some girl or skiving off school to go to the adult cinema down by the port. The poor woman found herself in a terrible pickle once, when her darling grandson got the pharmacist's daughter pregnant. Alejandro could scarcely have been fifteen at the time, and the girl nearly twenty. Can you imagine Doña Bevilacqua willing herself to stand, firm as an oak, in the face of gossiping neighbours?

I don't care what people say – I like the woman, even if we are separated by oceans and decades. I feel that both of us have had to deal with situations that were forced on us, and both of us have been prepared to fight tooth and nail to have something of our own in this life. She had to do it year after year. I did it every day. It's OK. God gives beans to the toothless.

I suppose, at the beginning, Alejandro must have won her over the way he did me. With the same allure, the same charm. She watched him grow, whereas I knew him as a grown man; but I'm sure both of us were captivated by his poise, his presence, that gift for warmth that came to him from somewhere deep inside. In my case, I don't know if it was the eyes, so deep you could drown in them, or those hands, which could make you shiver if you imagined them running over your skin, under your skirt... or the smooth neck into which you would love to sink your teeth... I'd better not go on.

I've always had a thing for older men. I mean, you're really sweet, Terradillos, but a bit too green for my taste. Come back to see me when you're riper. Alejandro was about fifteen years older than me – which, considering how young I was at the time, was quite some gap. The most handsome man I've ever known was my father, may he rest in peace. Look, there he is, in his silver frame, as befits a man like him. Did I tell you that my father was a bullfighter? I adored him.

On the evenings when there was a *corrida*, he, my mother and I would go to my paternal grandmother's house, because there was hot water there, and he could get ready more comfortably. My grandmother lived with two of her sisters, and these three old ladies would busy themselves with my mother, preparing his costume and laying out freshly laundered towels on the side of the bathtub, together with a perfumed soap that was kept for his exclusive use. My father would go into the bathroom and emerge after a while no longer himself but transformed into some magical creature, an enchanted being resplendent in pink silk embroidered with gold thread and sequins, and as handsome as the blessed St Stephen. We said goodbye to him ("never wish him luck," my mother warned me, when I was barely old enough to say anything), and I went to sit on the balcony between the geranium pots, with my legs hanging down either side of a post, to watch him as he left the house, and went, gleaming, down the cobbled street. Immediately my mother and her sisters put on their mantillas and took down from her niche Our Lady of Perpetual Help; my mother lit the candles, and the four of them set to reciting Hail Marys until his safe return.

They never went to see him *torear*, and they never dared turn on the radio during his absences. The hours passed, and I would either watch them pray or entertain myself looking at picture books until the moment came to return to my place on the balcony to witness his arrival at the end of our street, where the car left him, looking more real, more earthly now, but still as handsome as a count, perhaps with a trace of blood on his cheek, perhaps with a tear in his clothes, but never, thank God – as we had secretly feared – borne home on a stretcher, mortally wounded. He died when I was ten, from a pulmonary embolism, would you believe, of a tiny clot that had formed in some secret place in his veins and not, as I always imagined, losing streams of blood before his public. That's life. Look at him and tell me if you've ever seen anyone more handsome.

Don't imagine that Alejandro was like him. He wasn't, either in looks or temperament. The mere suspicion of blood made Alejandro queasy. He couldn't bring himself to step on an ant or shoo away a horsefly. I could never talk to him about bull-fighting; he went to pieces just at the idea of it. The mere thought of any action that might induce pain made him ill. He could never understand why anyone would want to fight. My father, on the other hand, understood it very well. My father was slender and graceful as a reed. Alejandro too was skinny, but he had flesh where it mattered. The first time I saw him at the Martín Fierro I thought, "Jesus, I'd gobble him up under the sheets," and I noticed that Quita wasn't exactly indifferent to him either. Because although she may have seemed very refined, the señora wasn't above singling out some refugee or other for her personal consumption. That Tito Gorostiza, for example, with his flowing hair and his black-leather shoulderbag – "an Andean hippy", Berens called him. And that Peruvian – I can't remember what he was called – who ended up living for a time in the cottage Quita had rented near Cáceres. Listen – I'm not accusing her of anything, all right? I think it's good for a woman to enjoy herself while she can.

But Alejandro was all mine. I told her that, right at the start, and Quita laughed and said of course, go for it. First we got him settled into Gorostiza's flat. Because Quita had put the flat in her boyfriend's name – a neat way of using the other tenants' rent to keep him, since selling trinkets on Calle Goya never appealed much to our Tito.

Alejandro, on the other hand, never complained about his lot. On the contrary, I would almost say that getting up every morning, gathering up his bracelets and rings, walking to his usual spot and spreading his wares out on the pavement gave him a certain security, I don't know – a fixed point in that nomadic life. After all, Alejandro was rather conservative. He liked good bed, good board, all that which can be savoured and stroked – indulgences that are hard to come by with your arse in the saddle. Ideally, he would have liked his mornings to follow a routine and his nights to be more adventurous. He would have made a good politician, my Alejandro.

But, what can I say, I'm nothing if not ambitious. To his other qualities I wanted him to add that of "artist". He may not have been keen to admit it, but Alejandro was so obviously a man of letters. I have a solid knowledge of South American writing – I don't know if you knew that. Ever since I was little, while my mother was devouring books by Gironella and

Casona (come to think of it, Carmen Laforet's *Nada* was on her bedside table too), I sought out authors from the other side of the Atlantic, whose books were sold under the counter by a few dedicated booksellers. Now, I wanted Alejandro to be one of them; I imagined him, undisputed and acclaimed, under one of those pastel-coloured covers with daring black letters which were produced at that time in Buenos Aires, standing aphabetically proud between Mario Benedetti and Julio Cortázar.

You know what? I wanted to be a part of that transformation which was slowly beginning to make itself felt throughout Spain, like a change of season, like the end of a long illness. Each one of us, I mean in my generation, experienced it in a different way, at different times. I can tell you that, for me, it was one day at school, at the end of class. I was about to leave the room when the headmistress, a very strict, formal woman, came in and told me to help her. She took one of the grey plastic wastepaper baskets that were in every classroom, and placed it in my hands. Then she lifted a chair onto the platform, pushed it over to the blackboard, unhooked the crucifix that had been hanging on the wall and put it into the wastepaper basket. We filled two baskets this way. Then we left them in a corner of the school chapel, under the astonished gaze of one of the priests who taught religious education. Sitting at my desk the next day, I felt for the first time freer, less stifled.

I wanted Alejandro to be a part of that wind of change, to be a dazzling new voice, a new discovery. Yes, yes, my Terradillos, I know what you're thinking: those fotonovelas of his were hardly literature. We had a laugh when he showed me three or four that he had discovered in a pile of old magazines in the Rastro flea market. Worse than soap operas – don't think I didn't realize that. I'm not stupid. But Alejandro knew the art of spinning stories. There was something about his tongue (I can see that you have a dirty mind from the way you're smiling), something in the way he measured words so well, with exactly the right nuances and shading, with more wisdom and delicacy than he ever showed stringing coloured beans together. People say that there used to be sorcerers in Andalusia who could make flowers and birds burst forth from the sky simply by naming them. Believe me, it was the same with Alejandro. When he told you something, you found yourself following his stories as if they were taking place in front of your own eyes; you could *see* it all happening. That was why it came as no surprise to me to learn that he had written a masterpiece.

Look, Terradillos. Compare him to anyone else. To Berens, let's say. Have you read any Berens, did you ever hear him reciting his stuff – before he went crazy, I mean? A prize for his first book, some other prize for the second. Here in Spain they loved him, because he was like a modern Bécquer. Even before the days when it became fashionable to award prizes to friends or because of publishing politics, everyone knew that the autumn wouldn't go by without Berens getting an award. But he was nothing compared to Alejandro.

I let him stay at Gorostiza's flat just for a couple of months, to get him acclimatized to Madrid. Because this was still, for the most part, a fearful city, cloaked, mute, drawn in on itself, not wanting to see anyone. When I was a young girl, I found it hard to believe that anything could ever bring down the great mountain of filth, of fetid candles and rotten vegetables bestowed on us by that dwarf, our Franco. I told myself that if Alejandro could cope with all that in a shared flat, my house was going to seem like paradise to him. That was how, one holiday weekend, I brought him back to live with me.

No doubt you've heard about how I found the manuscript. On several occasions I'd asked Alejandro to show me something that he had written, for I knew he *must* have written something; he had poetry in his blood. He always said no, that he wasn't a writer and I should leave him alone. I bought him a typewriter, hoping to tempt him. I left him on his own, gave him space, to see if solitude would stoke his inspiration. Nothing. He didn't take the typewriter out even once, and solitude seemed not to inspire him – at least not to write. In fact I once came home earlier than I had said I would and found him in bed with the Geisha from the flat next door (who I knew was a slut the day I saw her open the door with her kimono undone and her tits hanging out). Obviously I forgave him.

The thing is (forgive this digression), Alejandro had a vocation to share everything: food, readings, ideas, sex. If you put a plate of food in front of him, he insisted you try a little too. If he was reading a thriller, he'd call you over and read aloud some paragaph he liked. If an idea occurred to him in the middle of the night, some piece of nonsense, he'd wake you up to tell you about it. And, as far as he was concerned, a bed was not a place in which to sleep alone. He said that only selfish people masturbate.

One morning, when Alejandro had gone to his spot on Calle Goya, I found an old bag full of what looked like dirty washing. I opened it. There it was. *In Praise of Lying*, in clear, handwritten characters. There was no name on the title page, but I knew straight away what this was. I read it all the way through. It was hours later that I finished the last page, with tears in my eyes, I swear on the memory of my father, God bless his soul. There was something there, formed of vowels and consonants, to which the word "literature" scarcely does any justice. Even when you give it a capital "L".

I put all the things back as they had been and set off for the office with the manuscript. I called Urquieta, who must have thought that I wanted something else. I told him that I had to see him. He arranged to meet me in his café.

When I arrived, nervous and out of breath, Urquieta was already there, looking spruce in his hairpiece, and with a ready smile. He patted my wrist and insisted I tell him everything. I don't know if you ever spoke to Urquieta, but his voice was fatherly and measured, like a matinee idol's. It soothed me.

"I want to know what you think of this," I said, placing the novel under his nose.

"Is it yours?"

"It's a friend's"

"A friend. I see." And he smiled again.

"Read it," I answered, sternly. "Please. Read it."

"You're not asking me to whip through it now, in one sitting…"

"Make a start," I insisted, unflinching. "Later you can tell me what you think."

Perhaps he hoped to make a conquest; perhaps the role of wise counsellor appealed to him, or perhaps it was simply that he was an experienced reader who guessed that this effort would pay off. Urquieta obeyed. He placed his spectacles over his chubby nose, inspected the title page, commented on the calligraphy and colour of ink, looked, in vain, for the name of the author, discreetly adjusted his wig, turned the page and began to read.

No question about it: the man was a professional.

I didn't say a word. The waiter brought one coffee after another. Nearly an hour later, Urquieta looked up.

"Who wrote this?" he asked.

"First things first – what's your opinion?"

"Remarkable. From what I've read so far, very good. Excellent."

"A masterpiece – don't you think?"

"I don't know yet. I haven't finished it. And I'd have to read it at least once more."

"Señor Urquieta, I know that it is. I merely need you to confirm the fact."

"My dear, I need more information. Who is the author? How did this come into your hands?"

"Señor Urquieta, I can't tell you more than this. *In Praise of Lying* – I know that you don't doubt it – is a unique work, important, magical. We have to publish it. I mean, *you* have to publish it. You can give it the exposure it needs. You can give it the reputation it deserves. Do it – for the love of art, Señor Urquieta!" I let my voice grow sweet. "Future generations will thank you for it."

For some reason, Urquieta's eyes always appeared rather moist, as though he were constantly finding something funny or sad, and they also looked naked without the frame of eyelashes or eyebrows, like the eyes of certain old sheepdogs. Slowly, in the manner of a cautious buyer, he let his eyes run over the contours of my face, my neck, the curves of my blouse – and his imagination took care of the rest. It was well known that Urquieta liked to turn even the most banal or practical conversations into strategies of seduction, without much thought to the outcome. It was the chase he loved. If he found his companion even minimally attractive, Urquieta let his voice and gaze fondle her with lecherous impunity. Any discomfort this might cause didn't bother him in the least.

I let his eyes travel over me and watched him in turn, to see who would last longer. When pronouncing Ts and Ls, the old man let his tongue linger on his upper lip a fraction longer than was necessary, and there was an exaggerated pause before he answered my questions, fixing his gaze on some part of my body, as though staking claim to a territory. Several moments passed this way.

"For the love of art. Very well. Let's see. Leave the manuscript with me. Let's meet here again in three days. I'll give you my answer then."

Two days later I received a message at the Martín Fierro. It was Urquieta, summoning me back to the café.

His first words were: "We'll bring it out in three months. I'll send a copy to the eight people who count. I thought about having a launch in one of the cafés, the Lyon or the Ballena Alegre. But now I've thought of something better. A bookshop. We'll invite them to the Antonio Machado. We'll have a presentation like they do in Paris – make it a proper event. It's going to set the world on fire."

He put his hand on my arm. I don't mind confessing that I was genuinely grateful.

"You don't know how happy you've made me." And I added: "But I must warn you – the author knows nothing about this."

"He doesn't know that you've submitted it to me?"

"No."

"But then how will we do the contract? Who's going to sign it?"

"I'll sign it. I'll take responsibility."

"I don't like the sound of this. Why not let him know? Who is this elusive Pimpernel? What if he turns against us?"

But I also have my strategies. I knew that his bureaucratic instinct was no match for my charm.

"I know that you're not afraid of anyone," I said, smiling.

"Then I'm going to need your help."

"You can count on me," I said, with relief.

"Day and night," he said, smiling.

"Day and night," I agreed.

"And now tell me. Who is the author?"

"Bevilacqua. Alejandro Bevilacqua."

"The Argentinian? The one who shared a flat with Berens?"

"The very same. Now he shares mine."

"I see. And why does he not want his name to be known? We'll have to put it on the cover."

"Yes, of course – publish it, and he can find out about it then. But at the moment he doesn't even know that I've read it. The poor man was really traumatized by what he went through in Argentina. He insists that he isn't a writer, and yet here you have proof to the contrary. *In Praise of Lying* is going to give him a new start, I'm sure of it. A new life."

"Very well," concluded Urquieta. "We shall be the midwives at the birth."

Urquieta might be a vulture, but he was an intellectual too. "Birth" was the right word. Birth of the book, birth of the real, the secret Alejandro. I swear I was so happy, I almost threw myself on him, although Urquieta never needed any encouragement and he had already progressed from fondling my arm to slipping his fingers inside my sleeve and up between my dress and my armpit. But I didn't care. Alejandro was the writer I had always believed him to be.

Do you understand what I'm telling you, Terradillos, my inquisitive friend? He was a writer, a writer to the core, not like those others who passed through the Martín Fierro taking advantage of Quita's literary soft spot. They never were in the same league. I've been to countless poetry evenings, you know, when you had to keep an eye on the door, and also make sure that your poet didn't come out with some embarrassing remark or forbidden name – nothing that had a whiff of the Reds or Mother Russia. And even so, everyone would be waiting for some daring, blazing verse that would shine a light on us on those dark evenings. To no avail. God! To think of the times I must have listened to Berens – the most regular performer, of course, standing up on that little stage, in his imported suit, with his short, thin tie like a lizard's tongue pointing towards his navel, reciting his poems with a smile, as if he knew what they were about, while we, poor fools... Urquieta understood the difference perfectly. And he knew straight away that this was the real thing, a true fighting bull.

I'll spare you the technical details, the sealed bids, the hushed telephone conversations, Quita demanding to know what was going on (because nothing escaped that woman), Quita gossiping with Gorostiza, who was another curious creature, Quita swearing on St Christopher not to tell anyone anything, Berens finding out (I don't know how), more swearing, more devious plans, more secret meetings. And then, all the arguments about design, about the print runs, the cover – which was one of the first designed by the artist Max. And finally the proofs, the reality of the printed page, the title *In Praise of Lying* and the author's name, Alejandro Bevilacqua.

I remember that it was raining on the afternoon that Urquieta arranged to meet me, to hand over the first finished copy, wrapped in brown paper. I was shaking. The following morning, after serving Alejandro his coffee, I set the little packet down in front of him. Alejandro opened it, took out the book, looked at me, looked at the cover, opened the book, closed it, opened it again, closed it again, wrapped it back up in the paper and, leaving it on the table, picked up his things and went, without saying a word.

That day was the launch, and you already know what happened. Manguel was all over me, like a bad rash, and I had to let him take me to a café and then home, just to get him to leave me alone. Alejandro hadn't come home. I waited for him all that night and the following day.

It was Sunday. That day everyone filed through my house. Quita, with the excuse that she had lost the key to the till, Gorostiza like a one-man Inquisition (had anyone come to see Alejandro? Could he look through his papers for clues?), Urquieta, fatherly and solicitous. I told them time and again what I knew: why, how, where. Finally, at midday, I got rid of all of them and locked the door. A little later, Inspector Mendieta came to see me. It was he who broke the news to me.

You don't immediately understand something like that, even when it's explained to you clearly. You don't understand it, because you don't know how to understand it. You lack that space in your mind that would let you take it in. You are incapable of believing in the possibility of what they are telling you, because nothing of the sort has ever happened to you before. It is like a place that does not exist on your map of the world. You can't discover America if you have never told yourself that it could be there, on the other side of the ocean.

I spent the days that followed either in tears or asleep, expecting to see him walk through the door or to hear him calling from the other room. Sometimes I felt as though I had dreamt everything up: our meeting, our life together, our conversations between the sheets, the secret book.

The thing is, I don't know if these stories he was telling were mine, or his, or someone else's. You spend your life among words, listening, making sense out of what you say and out of what you imagine other people are saying to you, believing that something in particular happened like this or that, as a result of this or that, with these or those consequences. But it's never so simple, is it? I suppose that if we read about ourselves in a book, we wouldn't recognize ourselves, we wouldn't realize that those people doing certain things and behaving in a particular manner are us. I always believed that I knew Alejandro, that I knew him intimately, I mean, the way you might know a doll you've once taken to pieces. But it wasn't true.

Alejandro told me once about his crush on the girl puppeteer, back in Buenos Aires. He was very young then, and he had met that old German who made his living from puppet shows. The girl was his assistant, and Alejandro – who, even as a teenager, knew what he wanted – let the old man think he didn't mind having his bottom patted, his buttock squeezed occasionally, if it meant he could get closer to Loredana. In bed, he and the girl did everything, the works. Personally, I wouldn't have gone there, when you think what a baby Alejandro was at the time – I wouldn't even have taken my coat off for him. Loredana, on the other hand, was happy to go along with it and, while the old man spent hours untangling the strings on his puppets and eyeing up Alejandro, she would sit opposite the boy with her legs apart, her skirt rucked up and her knickers mislaid somewhere, or else she'd forget to do up a button on her shirt, showing her tits and some lacy edging against her coffee-coloured skin.

Alejandro could not stand to think of the girl going off without saying anything, and when he found out about her desertion he went after her to Chile. As I myself came to discover, on more than one occasion, Alejandro could not stand to be humiliated.

He told me that when he found her, in the restaurant room of that hotel, he treated her like a whore, in front of everyone. He described the things that they had done together. He threatened to go to the police. He accused the old man of corrupting her. He demanded money from them. Before returning to Buenos Aires, he gained access to the theatre dressing rooms and charged around like a bull in a china shop. He tore off the puppets' clothes and painted enormous dicks onto the wooden bodies.

I don't know if you'll understand this, but when Alejandro told me these things it wasn't by way of a confession. He told them in bed, while he was running his hands over my body. He told me because it excited him, I think, and he probably thought that it excited me too, to hear about it.

But to tell the truth, I hardly listened to him. I looked at him or, rather, I remembered him as he was that time I had first seen him in the Martín Fierro, feeling myself to be in love with him. I let my eyes travel over him, like someone travelling in the dark along a familiar road. I liked making mistakes, arriving at some unexpected part of his body, or confirming my hunch that this was a dark, passionate zone. I didn't mind if he wanted to tell me his life story – true or imaginary. I liked the sound of his voice, whatever it was saying. Not so much out of bed – but beneath the sheets everything is dreamlike. Whether or not these things had happened, or he simply believed them to have happened, was all the same to me.

I suppose Alejandro must have been like that with every woman. I haven't got a jealous bone in my body, so I can talk about these things without blushing. I don't think he was like that with Loredana, because he was not yet experienced with words, only with the body, which does its own thing. But certainly with his wife, with that Graciela, whom he never saw again. He didn't say as much to me about her, but I know that he yearned for that woman the way a person yearns to breathe. And especially so because someone had taken her from him, someone had deliberately handed her over to the executioners – you knew that? And this was something Alejandro never forgot. I imagine them to have been very similar, he and Graciela, like two consummate actors sharing a stage, with no false moves, not a word out of place, whether they were alone in bed or in the company of some extra, brought out from backstage to be the third leg in their irresistible double act.

He behaved differently with all the women he knew, myself included. I'm sure that those many other lovers, described to me night after night, hung on Alejandro's every word. To them he was like one of those storytellers who sit in the marketplace and mesmerize the crowd into silence. Enraptured, they would finally realize that the night had ended and that light was creeping in between the blinds.

Quita was the one who made me laugh. When I saw her come into the office in the mornings, I could have sworn on my life that she had been with Alejandro the night before. Not because the bastard hadn't come home, for that was a freedom he had demanded on our first day together, and which I had agreed to, or accepted – perhaps even wanted. But because Quita's skin had acquired an iridescent, silken quality, as though the words Alejandro had poured into her were still flowing through her blood, blue, golden and red. Gorostiza, who never would have admitted that he and Quita were a couple, watched her with a quiet, sad half-smile. I think that he voiced no reproach, so long as she allowed him to remain, clinging to her skirts, in the thick of things. Quita, on the other hand, was jealous – or perhaps "maternal" is a more precise term for those women who like to have a little man in their arms, close to the breast, like a Mater Dolorosa.

Alejandro lost his cool only once, that I remember. It was on a night that he came home late. He told me that he had met up with someone, but he didn't want to say who. He began to talk, hour after hour, without stopping. This time the aim was not to seduce anyone except perhaps himself, or to console himself, embolden himself. He began with that eternity spent in prison, about which he had already spoken to me, but this time it was as though he felt it in the flesh, as if he were reliving that hell through smell, touch, everyday objects. I don't know if I'm explaining this well: he was speaking across time.

They had picked him up in the way that had become standard at that time in Buenos Aires: the Ford Falcon drawing up to the pavement, the two men in dark glasses grabbing him by the shoulders, the blindfold across his eyes, the order not to touch the door handles, which were electrified. From beneath the blindfold he thought he recognized a street near the Recoleta cemetery. "The bus I took to school came this way," he thought then. And also: "If this had happened then, from my seat I would have seen myself being taken away, because I always looked out on this side."

When they came to some invisible gates, one of the men took down the car radio and uttered what must have been the code to open them. "Uranus". That was the first word of a new vocabulary that Alejandro had to learn during his confinement, as though his past life had suddenly been erased and he were starting again in some monstrous school where ghostly hands wrote cryptic terms on the blackboard in a tidy hand: *operating theatre*; *the machine*; *the grill*; *the egg cup*; *the lion's den*; *the hood*; *the kennel*; *the tube*; *the cabin*; *the lorry*; *the flights*; *the fish food*; *the fish tank*. Take this down, Terradillos, because it's history and evidence. I'm telling you this just as he told me, sparing you only the ins and outs. You see: no secrets.

He spent the first days sitting on the floor, with nothing to lean against, unable to move, as rigid as a bullfighter in the veronica stance, with the blindfold tight across his eyes. He learnt to look downwards, to recognize the guards' voices, to intuit the presence of others. He thought he knew that the cell was large and that he was not its only occupant. At irregular intervals he heard the door open and close, and felt someone place a bowl of soup in his hands, or a glass of water. In the middle of the room there was a pit for relieving himself. Some time afterwards, he learnt that the building was known as The Cesspit.

After three or four days, two men came into the cell and removed the blindfold. They took him, blinking in the light, to a room that looked like an office and was immaculately tidy. They made him sit on one side of a desk and, without saying a word, settled themselves on the other, under a portrait of General San Martín. After a while they brought him a chair. Two or three hours passed this way, in silence. Then the pair got up, went to the door and ushered in two other men, who were almost identical and took over from the first. This game continued, without words or variations, for nearly a week. Sometimes Alejandro fell asleep on top of the desk, or with his head lolling back against the seat, and then one of the men would stand up and slap his face. Every ten or twelve hours, a woman in an apron brought him something to eat and drink. Alejandro ate and drank and tried to sleep with his eyes open. Nobody said a word.

We know the game in which the threat is never voiced but the imagination is left to build its own hell, in which the fear of what can happen lends a face and claws to a monster that always remains inside your mind. A promise of something unspoken. A curtain raised with no one entering the stage. Allowing the squeak of a door to be heard, or the lash of a belt, the scraping of metal in the darkness. You can imagine it all, can't you?

We know about it. Writing, Terradillos, is a kind of silence, of not speaking, of shooting words down mid-flight, as the poet Vallejo once said, of rooting them on the page. Writing is a way of threatening what is not spoken aloud; the shadow of the letters taunts us from between the lines. I am too much a lover of Latin American fiction not to be accustomed to aphony, to reticence, to silence. Will you allow me a reader's aside? From the start, under the pretext of describing great spaces and narrating vast epics, South America's chroniclers set out to suggest certain key ideas, to leave a few faint traces. They staged some epic dramas, for sure, novel after voluminous novel, but at the end of the day the story's essence boiled down to a few words hidden beneath the load of some impetuous paragraph we almost didn't read, so distracted were we by number of pages. Sometimes they are concealed in the dialogue, in a footnote, perhaps even in the title. The rest would be superfluous, except that it serves to hide what really matters. It is, as those erudite Anglo-Saxons claim, a "literature of violence", but less political than metaphysical, less in the flesh than intellectual. It concerns itself not so much with obvious violence as with the other, the deliberate, insidious kind. The wound beneath the blow, the offence beneath the insult, the mask behind another mask, the one everyone recognizes. Believe me. Lying: that is the great theme of South American literature.

Alejandro told me that, when they finally began to beat him, the pain almost came as a relief. Hour after hour, day upon day, he had allowed himself to dream up the most atrocious tortures, the most unbearable agonies. Steel, fire, water, lack of air – he had conjured up all of it before actually feeling it in the flesh. He who couldn't even bear you to step on a caterpillar, to hurt a cat, was made to imagine everything. And later on, the things that he had imagined began to happen, but differently.

One of the men who often came back to visit him had, Alejandro told me, very soft, smooth skin, like a woman's. He knew this not because he could see him (the man never entered his cell except when Alejandro's eyes were bandaged), but because every time he came, he took Alejandro's hand in his own, as though he were a gypsy about to tell his fortune. Then, when they led him, with shackled feet and tied hands, to the little room where one of the surgeons (that's what they were called) had to do his job, Alejandro had the impression that the man with soft skin was still there, watching him, always quiet, always sad. Alejandro imagined him as one of Loredana's puppets, which, skewered on its stick, could only swivel from left to right, swaying its arms, rigid, with fixed glass eyes and varnished cheeks reflecting the footlights. In his cast of monsters, he gave this ghostly individual the name Muñeco, meaning "doll". He told me that this character obsessed him to such a degree that, a few days after arriving in Madrid, he thought he heard Muñeco's voice in a café, in a shop, even at the Martín Fierro. Apparently many people experience this kind of hallucination, even months after leaving their own individual hells.

Alejandro did not know what they asked him, nor what he answered during the time he spent in this first cell. He had a confused recollection of beatings, shouting, terrible silences, expressionless faces, gobs of spit, the cries of men and women on the other side of the wall, the pain of injuries he could not see, moments of light sleep, almost without nightmares, the lights constantly lit, a craving for darkness, thirst. At some point they told him that Graciela was dead; later they said that she wasn't, that she had shacked up with one of the surgeons; later that she was being tortured in a distant cell. I don't know if he ever discovered the truth.

He had the sensation of separating himself from himself, or splitting into two and feeling that it was his double who was there, lying or sitting, expectant or expecting nothing. He said that it was during those endless months that he began to have the impression of living at the edge of real time, a feeling that never left him completely. When I first met him, sometimes he would wake up saying that he had seen himself stretched out by my side, as though he were dead.

One day, without explanation, they moved him to a cell with only two camp beds. In one corner there was a lavatory with no seat and a washstand. To be accorded such luxuries astonished him. Alejandro recalled how he had not felt water run over his skin for a long time. They left him alone, but it was ages before he allowed himself to go to the basin and turn on a tap. The freezing water made him weep with joy.

They say that intense cold slows the rhythm of the body, reducing the heart rate and pressure of blood in the veins. During those weeks, Alejandro's senses had grown less acute, his perception dimmer. It was hours before he registered the presence of someone in the second camp bed. Only when a booming voice asked him his name did he realize that there was somebody of flesh and blood there. Quite a lot of flesh: El Chancho, "The Pig", as Alejandro called him (he never told me his real name), was a man of such low stature, or rather of such short arms and legs that, in spite of his enormous torso and bulging belly, he resembled a dwarf. His one charm (if you can talk of charm in such a graceless creature) was his voice. El Chancho was loquacious. Alejandro, on the other hand, feared that he might have forgotten how to talk altogether.

It wasn't long before Alejandro discovered that El Chancho seemed to have some curious links with the authorities. He was a prisoner, certainly, but a prisoner with benefits, you might say. With the exception of one almighty beating he had received on first entering The Cesspit (about which he gave Alejandro all the gory details), the guards had not so much as touched a hair on his head, and even conceded him countless small favours. Sometimes they brought him magazines and books, which El Chancho discreetly shared with Alejandro, sometimes special food, which he kept to himself. They also allowed him paper and a biro, and El Chancho spent hours filling the sheets with writing in an even, clerical hand, very similar to Alejandro's. He had a wife, as tall as he was short and as skinny as he was fat, who was known as La Pájara and whom El Chancho adored with the fervour of a man possessed. Every so often, El Chancho was let out of the shared cell and taken to another one where La Pájara had been brought, and there they spent the night together.

In that world, La Pájara was simply one in a cast of peculiar beings. In a miniskirt that drew attention to her rather full behind bouncing along on top of long legs, with her hair gathered up in the style of a turban and crowned with some outlandish hat, with her lips painted a communist red, La Pájara would arrive in the evenings with a little packet of sweets, as though she were visiting a convalescent. The only visits Alejandro was permitted, meanwhile, were from an older woman, dressed as a nurse, who took his pulse, and a young, melancholic priest who spoke to him of the Good Shepherd. These people came to see him as he lay in a state of confusion, after the really heavy sessions, when, having been dragged down corridors with signs that proclaimed "Happiness Avenue" or "Silence Is Healthy" he would be left on the camp bed, bound hand and foot. Compared to them, the obese dwarf and the tall woman seemed unreal, or at least as unlikely as the other strange inhabitants of that world in which he did not wish to believe.

After he was transferred to El Chancho's cell, Alejandro's sessions with the surgeons gradually became less frequent and finally stopped altogether. He never knew why. A diabolical law governs places like The Cesspit, with its own rules and geometry. Now the days and nights became long periods of pointless waiting in which he did not know whether to fear the morning or long for it. In the meantime, El Chancho seemed increasingly eager to show him a kind of affection or complicity. He spoke to Alejandro of the sweet perfume of Havana, the milk-coffee colour of the Caribbean coastline, of long evening readings on the terrace of some famous novelist's home and of long nights partying on a still, warm beach. He recalled books for Alejandro (because it seems that El Chancho was a great reader); he told him about writers he had known in his youth; he invented stories with details which he developed and embroidered day after day. Of their own situation, he said very little. "Let us invent the world, brother," El

Chancho would say. "This one doesn't really exist." And, after a moment he added, laughing: "Or ought not to exist, at any rate!"

One afternoon, El Chancho returned to the cell after a short "informative" session, and told Alejandro that La Pájara would not be coming any more. He said that the surgeons, after reeling off countless numbers and dates which El Chancho claimed not to remember, had blindfolded him and put a hood over his head. Then he had heard the door of the little room open, and the soft voice of Muñeco told him that their patience had come to an end and, with it, the privileges. He shouldn't expect a visit from his wife that night, or ever again.

And slowly, in fine detail, Muñeco explained what had happened to La Pájara. El Chancho refused to believe it. He prepared himself to wait. That night passed and the one following. Alejandro didn't dare speak to him. El Chancho neither ate nor slept. He kept his eyes on the door of the cell, as though the slightest distraction on his part could cause a fragile apparition to vanish.

Some time later, one of the other prisoners managed to whisper in El Chancho's ear that there had been a shoot-out near The Cesspit, that a car carrying several women had been set ablaze. El Chancho passed from depression to anger, then from anger to an animal fury, punching the walls and howling like a wolf and – even after three guards had softened him up – he was still fuming. Finally they took him away.

At the same time, the surgeons resumed their sessions with Alejandro. One day, after a particularly violent session that left him with a constant ringing in his ears, which were already sensitive after the demonstration in Buenos Aires ("as though I were in the midst of a thousand bell towers," he once told me), Alejandro was sitting on his bed with his feet still tied and his eyes bandaged when he heard Muñeco's voice speaking to him. "I came to say goodbye," said Muñeco. "Perhaps we'll see each other again. If we don't die first, you or I."

The seven or eight months Alejandro spent at The Cesspit left its mark on his memory – and on his arms and legs – for years. Suddenly everything ended in as inexplicable a fashion as it had begun. A week after El Chancho was taken away, a couple of strangers entered the cell and ordered Alejandro to leave it. They blindfolded him once more, tied his feet and hands, led him down the familiar corridors and through the hellish gates and put him in a car. "It was as if they were running the film backwards," he told me. "I had the impression that everything was about to start again."

After an hour, the car stopped. They removed the shackles, the ties and the blindfold; they placed a bag in his hands and told him to get out. Overhead, several planes were drawing furrows through the sky. The next day, Alejandro landed at Barajas Airport, in Madrid. Who would have imagined it? Now we know that the feet that trod Spanish soil for the first time that day would lead him irrevocably to the fateful balcony.

But what a question, Terradillos! You have to remember that this happened three decades ago. There is an infinite distance between the twenty-five-year-old girl I was then and the half-century me of today. I get the sequence of events muddled up, you know, like in a badly shuffled pack of cards. I can no longer say for sure exactly when I heard about Alejandro's death, whether Quita told me about it that same day, or if, on seeing me come into the Martín Fierro, the poor woman sent me away, shouting like a lunatic that he was dead, he was dead. Perhaps someone had already told me – Berens, I think – that there were two deaths, because Tito Gorostiza had also taken his life. Or it could have been Inspector Mendieta, who came to see me once again, asking more questions than there are in the catechism, until I ended up not knowing what either of us was talking about. I can no longer remember which things I imagined and which

I knew for sure, which stories I was told and which I wove myself, in an effort to figure things out.

Later it came to matter less. The world changed. When Quita fell ill, poor thing, she called me, but we didn't talk about what had happened. Berens was probably the one who came out of things best, forever isolated by his Alzheimer's. Perhaps we get used to everything in the end, even oblivion.

Sometimes I am haunted by an image from those days, and it's as if I see myself in a mirror as I was when Alejandro loved me. Look at me now! But in those days, this body was still attractive and this mind was sharper and quicker. I don't care what wise men say – age does not sharpen our senses, it deadens them. We need keen *banderillas* to get us going after fifty. That's what my father always said, and nowadays I find myself agreeing with him.

As far as you and your readers are concerned, Terradillos, Alejandro's story holds no surprises now. The facts have been established to the satisfaction of the coroner and the dossier closed with the seal of the Archangel Gabriel. *In Praise of Lying* hasn't been seen for years, unless it's in the window of an antiquarian bookshop, with a hefty price tag attached. A small publishing house here wanted to reprint it, but it was impossible to reach an agreement with some incompetent heirs who didn't want to have anything to do with it. It's for the best. That whole episode was embarrassing enough without having to live through it again.

I still read literature from Alejandro's homeland. I still seek traces of him in the books that reach us from the antipodes. I still believe that one day I'll uncover the proof that my intuition was not wrong, that under the man everyone else thought they knew was hidden a novelist, a poet.

I know that we are all fools in love, that we let ourselves create plausible ghosts in place of our loved ones. Or rather, we create a ghost which enters the solid person we see in front of us, inhabiting him, looking back at us from behind his eyes. And with the certainty that this creature is our beloved comes another certainty: that we shall never forget him, that we shall never betray him, that he will be for ever at the centre of our lives, of everything that is ours, however unlikely a figment he is.

I'm going to tell you something, but you must keep it to yourself, because it's silly and I'm a little embarrassed to say it. Some time ago, in the window of a second-hand bookshop, I saw a collection of poems: the author's name was A. Bevilacqua. I went in, bought it, hurried to a café and sat down to read it. The title was something like *Counterflows* or *Cross-currents*. It was light, romantic verse, with a lot of exclamation marks and capital letters. I flicked anxiously through it, unsure exactly what I was looking for, but wanting to hear Alejandro's sombre tones, to feel his hands on the nape of my neck, the smell of his tobacco in my nostrils. I thought I recognized the cadence of his sentences, his measured way of looking at things; I was surprised to see an epigraph from an author I didn't know he liked. When I had finished the last poem, I turned back to the first. I looked for a date in the copyright page: my edition had been printed at the end of 1990s in Montevideo, but the first publication was in 1961; Alejandro would have been about twenty years old then. I read the book a third time and came, once more, to the imprint page. Only then did I spot something I hadn't seen, or hadn't wanted to see before: the author's name was indeed Bevilacqua, but Andrés, not Alejandro. This was an unknown Andrés Bevilacqua, homonymous usurper of my writer, a false prophet, false ghost, with a false voice and false touch. I felt my mistake as an unforgiveable betrayal, a violation of his memory. I, who had loved him so much, had been disloyal. I left the book on the café table and went back home, distraught.

I once read somewhere that the only thing we can do to fight against the unreality of the world is to tell our own story. I have never wanted to do that.

I prefer to redeem him and what I knew or believed I knew of him. It doesn't matter to me much if the truth turns out to be otherwise. You, my Terradillos, must write what you think best, and time will tell.

Alejandro was whatever I felt or imagined him to be during the time that we knew each other. If I am still looking for proof of my conviction, it's out of habit or need. Does that make sense? My father said that if you have spent years in a bullring, you continue to wield the cape in your dreams, even when nothing is left around you: no bull, no spectators, no sand.

That's how it is. Without a doubt.

3

THE BLUE FAIRY

"Be honest and good and you'll he happy,"
the Fairy told him.

Carlo Collodi
The Adventures of Pinocchio

Monsieur Jean-Luc Terradillos,
L'Actualité Poitou-Charentes
Poitiers, France

1st January 2003

My dear Curious Impertinent,

I mistrust letters as a literary genre. They claim to tell an impartial truth independent of their scrumdolious author (my Cuban grandmother used this adjective to describe dresses which look swanky but are badly cut and sewn, and I bet myself that I would manage to use it in the first paragraph), when the opposite is true: only one chronicler gets to give his version of the story. But the epistolary genre is, in this case, the only one left to me. I've exhausted all my options: my literature no longer encompasses the epic genre, and the lyric one, such a conceited form, has always been denied to my muse. So I'll have to be satisfied with this letter. At least no shit-stirring editor is going to stick his nose in it.

I met Bevilacqua in prison, but you already know that. I enjoyed talking to him, telling him my repertoire of stories, bouncing my literary inventions off his beleaguered eardrums. Whenever I start remembering things, my lips move of their own accord. If I have a typewriter in front of me, I start typing; if I have a blank page, I start writing; in the absence of any other instrument, I use my tongue. At night, faced with sheep butchers that get in the way of sleep, I make up stories that begin to unravel as I fall into the darkness. Bevilacqua was good for that: he could stop them unravelling.

Right from the beginning I trusted him. I felt that I could trust him the way that, in the army, one instinctively trusts the less daring corporal, the more familiar weapon. Novelty is no friend to success. And for someone like me, whose attractions are not obvious, it's better not to expect aesthetic charity from anyone. Sincerity, yes, that's a different matter. Or honesty, which brings with it a touch of meekness.

He wasn't jealous. That envy which fuels literary inspiration, which desires that every one else's books fail and all their recompense be derisory – that wasn't apparent in Bevilacqua. His emotions were all on the surface; envy requires a pretence of modesty, a show of reserve, and reveals itself at the corners of the mouth, in the hue of one's skin. Bevilacqua's smile was sweet, and his skin a constant grey. Of course prison would not have put colour in his cheeks even if his constitution had favoured it. As the Good Book puts it, "when I was in my Father's house, I was in a better place".

It's weird how the most humdrum places can produce encounters that go on to have momentous consequences. For him, in this case, not for me. Human beings can be divided between those whom the gods, for their own amusement, guide through strange woods only to abandon them somewhere at the edge of a precipice, on a moonless night, and the others who find their own way along well-lit paths. I never lost my way. Whether I was filling a book with letters or a suitcase with banknotes, I was always disciplined; I always knew what I was doing. It isn't true that certain constellations and propitious winds must be in place for our destiny to be fulfilled: all that is required is a solid punt and someone to row it. That's important: some poor, obedient soul.

Bevilacqua served my purpose, without my realizing it at the time.

I think, in some ways, my fate has been dictated by my physique. My nickname isn't merely a nickname; I resigned myself early on to acknowledging it as a *nom juste*. The other one, bestowed on me at baptism, is the misnomer. Nobody who looks like me can rightly be called Marcelino Olivares. No one. As a boy, and a devoted reader of Pinocchio, I realized that I was my own caricature, the reverse of my hero: a little boy converted into an ugly lump of wood. That had its advantages: it was impossible to laugh at me, because I was already too much of a buffoon. One can't parody a parody. Short arms, truncated legs, a barrel chest and a face better shaped for disgust than for desire – that's me. My face, in particular, is like something a romanesque sculptor would place in the buttresses of churches to chase off the devil. Not that I would have wanted to have one of those gentle, light, angelic faces blandly adorning the columns inside. But perhaps something in between. It doesn't matter much, because the conditional tense doesn't get you far. The thing is that, with looks like mine, it was clear that only two careers were open to me: arms and letters. I dedicated myself to both.

When I was twenty years old I went to enlist under the severe gaze of General Batista, whose portrait adorned every room in every office. The sergeant who took my details asked if I would prefer to be known as El Chancho, "The Pig", or El Sapo, "The Toad". I don't know why I chose the former – perhaps because the porcine race is more associated with the world of smells and that of batrachians with touch.

To this brief self-portrait I've sketched for you, I must add one last disagreeable feature: my sense of smell. One day, during my adolescence, I woke up in the middle of a terrible stench. I looked for the cause and, unable to find it, I asked my mother what it was that smelt so bad. That was how I found out that the smell did not exist for other people – only, by divine grace, for me. Certain molecules in my chemical make-up communicated to my mind the impression of a constant stink, an olfactive hallucination, a fetid phantasm that did not exist for anyone else. I live with it. They say that the emperor Germanicus suffered from the same ailment. As for me, I have grown so accustomed to its presence (given that more than sixty years of doctors and healers have not been able to cure my disease) that I have given it a name: it's called Rubén, after my father. Rubén inhabits my nasal day and night. I am never alone.

Do you believe in reincarnation? I do. I believe that this flesh, this brain, these stubby fingers will fall to ashes, but also that the imagination contained in this flesh, this brain, these fingers will be reconstituted in some other form that I still don't know. An ant-eater, for example, something that would make sense of my nasal encumbrance. A fat, short-legged spider, spinning patterns with its own saliva, as I did with my writing. Or, why not, a tree, strong and squat, throwing roots down into the shit, like a profusion of Ys – *yaicuaje*, *yagruma*, *yaití*, *yaba* – the trees that twist and delve into my native land. Rubén would like that, living in a swamp.

What would my Basque grandfather have made of his horrifying grandson? Eliades Cemi Olivares arrived in Cuba in the nineteenth century, trailing along his younger brother, Miguel. With pleasing symmetry, Eliades and Miguel married Martina and Socorro, two little sisters from Camagüey, more black than mulatto, who gave them litters of children at nine-month intervals. My father was one of the middle-rankers in a long line of progeny scattered across the island.

Perhaps it was a contrary nature, rather than any repulsion he may have felt on seeing me, that prompted my father to limit his own progeny to only one. He did not love me. That absence of love may have explained his parsimonious seed-sowing; the kicks and punches that characterized our relationship would seem to confirm this theory. My mother would beg him not to kill me; my father obeyed, stopping on that threshold that separates the body present from the absent soul. My mother really did love me. I listened at her knee as she told me that in a few years I would be like other boys, and with the patience of a hummingbird she attempted to kiss me on my almost inexistent nape, between my outsize ear and my enormous shoulder. Her promise of normality was never fulfilled, of course. But learning to live on the margins of normal life served me well later on, when, in times of hardship, I was tempted to take the lazy option and call it a day. I learnt not to suffer from vertigo.

I joined the Cuban army very young, just as it was beginning to fight the rebels in the Sierra. At that time this was not yet a serious enterprise, although (probably to frighten us) the colonel, an enthusiast of war films, handed to each conscript a little yellow-and-black capsule which he said contained cyanide, and which we must break open with our teeth should we fall into enemy hands. That capsule, which I christened my "bee", accompanied me through many years, from one enemy to the next.

Our mission, when we weren't drinking or groping each other back at base, was to ambush the rebels who came down from the mountains to steal food and munitions. We called this "the vermin hunt", and we placed bets on who could snare a peasant first. Few of us ever won. At night they sent us out to patrol the streets, so that the American marines could finish their puddings in peace at the Miami Prado or the Neptune, or to shoo away from street corners any troubled soul who might otherwise be found hanging from a lamp-post the next morning. There's nothing like dawn in Havana.

I have no talent for hunting. When they sent us on those missions, I stayed in the rearguard, letting myself be swept along by the column of handsome, smiling boys. Once we came to some hovel on the beach, where they had told us we would find a peasant who had stolen two pigs from a farm nearby. A small, dark-skinned woman came out, frowning. "What are you looking for?" she asked before we could say anything. "Severo Frías," answered our sergeant. "He's not here." "And who are you?" "His mother." "We're going to come in and look for him." The woman fixed us with a furious look. "I've told you, he isn't here." "We're coming in all the same, Señora. Just to be sure." "Well, then take off your boots. I've just washed the floor, and I'm not having you make it dirty again with those filthy shit-boots." The sergeant ordered us to remove our boots. When we made to enter the house, the woman stopped me. "Not this one," she said to the sergeant. "He's going to jinx the house." I waited outside while my fellow soldiers carried out their search. They found nothing. I never told the sergeant that, while they were putting their boots back on and taking leave of the woman, I saw a pair of eyes shining beneath the veranda. Before we left, I looked at the woman and smiled. She was still scowling.

I left Cuba a little before Dr Castro's first skirmishes, in one of those boats that depart amid streamers and arrive to trumpets and balloons. I'm not heroic. As I've said, my twin-headed vocation was for arms and letters: yes, but neither to get killed, nor to bend over to a publisher's prurience. Our duty in this life is to survive, not to die. In that sense, the military attitude is right. (The true one, not the one which sends poor chancers out on the front line like those sacrificial goats which hunters in Johnny Weismuller films place in pits to snare tigers.) To identify an enemy, plan an attack, predict a line of defence, devise a withdrawal strategy. That was how I turned up at the Cuban embassy in Buenos Aires, in the summer of 1952.

Do you know what it's like to fall in love? It's like entering another state, an all-encompassing cosmography. Not the dream of love, which we say will arrive one day or which we believe, in spite of everything, to be living in the present. Not the conviction of an attractive exterior, the rational justification of an ecstasy. I mean absolute captivity, heart and mind – unconditional, irrevocable surrender. The blinding revelation: *I no longer belong to myself, I am hers entirely, I live because she lives, and I live only for her.* I compare it to a translation. All of me in another language, everything I am to be read now through her language, which I must learn, as I once learnt my ABC. *I shall know who I am when I know who she is.* That is what I am talking about.

The daughter of our commercial attaché was about seventeen at the time. During dinners at which the ambassador liked to surprise his guests – who had never suspected such Caribbean formality – with detailed menus in elegant French calligraphy, Bohemian porcelain bowls, filled to the brim with gorgeous fruit, silver cutlery arrayed in decreasing sizes to the right and left, and fancy wines poured into Baccarat glasses, I amused myself telling the girl stories of cannibals, of wild men whose heads grew beneath their shoulders. I seduced my Desdemona with my voice.

It may surprise you to know that I am a man not much given to change. I obey conventions. In general, I write according to the rules of the Royal

Spanish Academy, which are the same as those of the Cuban Academy of the Language, and no worse than any others. My sentences all come with verbs, my subjects have a predicate, my pronouns know how to differentiate the accusative from the dative. I wear a tie. I never sit down to eat in short sleeves. I don't work on Sundays. I married Margarita soon after her eighteenth birthday, both of us still virgins. My mother-in-law wept. Several times during the celebrations I heard her whisper: "He's the ugliest man I've ever seen."

My new family extended to me, among other things, various privileges: a genteel house near the Bosque de Palermo in Buenos Aires, a lowly position at the Embassy (revoked in that fatal year of 1959); introductions to various writers and other creatures of the publishing world and, above all, good contacts with a range of Argentine military types who had acquired a certain notoriety after the flight of General Perón. I knew how to make the most of this. Bridges must be built between the Arts and the Arms. We know (because we have read it in *Don Quixote*) that to be eminent in the Arts requires time, vigilance, nakedness, mental confusion, indigestion and other things; to be eminent in Arms entails all this plus a risk of death. I accept that this is the way things are, although I haven't had to try it myself. Therefore I pressed my literary experience (to say nothing of time, vigilance, etc.) into the service of the army. The military needed stories: I provided them.

The problem, as with almost all the problems of those who hold power, was simple. On the other side of the law (I mean, on the side of those who lack and desire that power) there exists a solid parallel economy. Shady deals, bribes, cash collections, interest, bankruptcies and fortunes are made and unmade on thatmurky Wall Street. When the two sides come face to face (which happens less frequently than one might suppose) and the powerful side wins (also less common than moralists would have us believe), the rules of the engagement demand that secret fortunes change hands. Were such covert dealings to come to light, it would cause a worse stink than my poor Rubén; it would stir up decades' worth of sludge, unearthing skeletons and putrefaction which nobody wants to remember. In such cases, ideally one would appoint a Charon, accustomed to darkness and willing to ferry these ghostly monies from the side of the living to that of the immortal – the Swiss, for example. I offered my services, with discretion. With discretion, the military men accepted. I could have pictured them, wearing their autumn uniforms, stretching out their hands full of love, towards the other bank.

For years, as one government was succeeded by the next, I served as Charon for these high-ranking gentlemen, carrying, for a modest commission, sums that were invisible to the public eye, from a safe in La Plata or Córdoba to the near-anonymous coffers of certain European banks. I was efficient, punctual, modest and reliable. Superstitious too: my bee talisman was always in my pocket, just in case. I never made a mistake: I never arrived late, I never opened my mouth, I never forgot anything. I carried out my duties with the same rigour I applied to writing. There are no real synonyms in business or literature. Nothing is "as if".

At the start of the new decade, a new, unprecedented source began to swell the contents of my saddlebags, or rather the saddlebags in my care. The "subversives" (as they were known to my clients) were now using kidnapping and holding up banks as a way to procure funds; with increasing regularity, these funds ended up in the gloved hands of a colonel, an admiral or a general. My job was to channel the funds. I did so with my – by now proverbial – diligence. Only, this time, I decided that greater danger deserved greater recompense. Without wishing to bother the gentlemen with a trivial enquiry, I took what (in my opinion) I was entitled to and, having a knack for the craft of fiction, spun a story to justify the figures. Three or four times, everything worked wonderfully. The fifth time was different. An over-scrupulous colonel did a few sums. At the airport, on the way back from Geneva, an immigration officer asked me to accompany him. All night they beat the soul out of me, demanding to know the number of the secret bank account. At dawn I gave it to them. It never occurred to them that there were two accounts. I spent several weeks in that place – I don't want to remember its name – hooded and shackled, naked on the floor as lurid folk music resounded incessantly around the four windowless walls. Before going to sleep, I put paper in my ears to keep the cockroaches out. Those days left me with a fear of bright lights: that is why I always wear dark glasses.

During my abduction (the word "detention" does not do justice to the physical violation I suffered), it crossed my mind that perhaps some literary angel would notice my absence. Nobody did. The list of supposed friends who took my disappearance as proof of my non-existence is long. It had been years since I had last had links with the Embassy, where ruffles had been replaced with beards and the portrait of Batista with one of the heroes of the Revolution – with no sign of a slow-down in the consumption of oysters and champagne. My editor (because I had one, Gastón Asín Hajal, a pornographer by vocation and a usurer by practice – I wish him a painful death) gave the order for my books to be pulped on the sly so as to leave no trace of my presence in his catalogue.

Treachery has its artists. Polybius, in one of the few surviving pages of a work which has been lost for the most part, says that it is not easy to establish who can properly be considered a traitor. According to him, the name cannot be applied to a man who freely puts himself at the service of certain monarchs or regents in order to do their bidding, nor to him who, in extreme circumstances, incites his fellow citizens to break old alliances or friendships in order to forge new ones. Polybius seems to reserve this opprobrious title for the man who benefits from his own actions: the person who denounces a friend in order to save himself, or who hands over the keys to a city to advance personal ambitions. My traitors (with one exception, but I'll talk about him later) were more subtle. They simply did nothing. Hajal denied knowing me. This flaccid cocaine addict for whom Apelles's motto *nulla dies sine linea* – not a day without a line – could have been justly written, presented himself now as a virtuous prude. He came over all forgetful, claiming that my grotesque figure had been erased from his literary memory and that, in any case, an editor such as he had neither the obligation nor the resources to help every pen-pusher who had, at some time, borne his imprimatur.

Theology teaches us that, of all sins, those of omission are the most interesting and complex. Having always written in secret and been almost obsessively discreet, I handed to my friends the justification for their own treachery. They were all able to claim that my disappearance was nothing out of the ordinary, but the obvious and predictable result, by now of common knowledge, of my ill-defined presence.

I suspect that there are many of us spinning in the shadows. My books were not published, with the exception of a few anthologies of other people's work, the odd short story and an ill-fated novel to which Hajal added an obscene title and one or two anatomically exaggerated descriptions. It enraged me to see the windows of bookshops filled, month after month, with disgusting novelties that oscillated beween hyperbolic pretension or documentalist fervour. Hajal, to whom I confided some of my feelings, told me with a smile that the name of that fury was envy. He was right, up to a point. Apparently, during a soirée at which Oscar Wilde was present, one of the topics of conversation was literary jealousy. Wilde told the following story. The

Devil sent several demons to tempt a very saintly hermit. The demons tried everything, but not even the most delicious food, the most beautiful women or the greatest riches were capable of distracting the hermit from his prayers. Impatient, the Devil told his followers: "That's not how you do it – watch and learn." And, approaching the holy man, he whispered in his ear: "Your brother's been made Archbishop of Alexandria." Immediately the old man's face contorted with a grimace of furious envy.

So you see, that envy, that fury (which, as I said before, were foreign to Bevilacqua), I cultivated patiently. I'm convinced that it is a good cordial for the imagination and, at the end of the day, an excellent remedy for taking revenge on life. I think it's not too far-fetched to say that I kept my fury alive with deliberate elegance – if one can speak of elegance in someone with my appearance.

Perhaps it was this fighting fire with fire that gave me, during those terrible days, the patience and the heart necessary to survive and also, paradoxically, the hope that my situation would change. And so it was. Nothing in my circumstances pointed towards this change except for my burning desire, and I am convinced that desire shapes our reality. If something does not happen, it is because we failed to desire it with sufficient force.

One day, I was moved to the building they called The Cesspit. Torture was practised there too, of course, but, alongside the dungeons where business was carried out there were cells that were more or less (I hesitate to use the epithet) comfortable. I was put into one of these. Perhaps as a reward for having given them the bank-account number, perhaps because one of those sinners thought he would salve his conscience by awarding me a stint in limbo, or perhaps (more likely), in the topsy-turvy logic of that system, somebody had judged that a given act of contrition deserved a corresponding privilege. Suddenly I could wash myself, use lavatory paper, eat something recognizable, sleep under a blanket, sit at a table without shackles or a hood, protect my eyes once more with dark glasses, receive books to read and paper to write on. Amazingly, they allowed Margarita to visit me. I asked her to bring my "bee", just in case, although I knew that I would never succumb to using it. Our understanding of Paradise can only be defined by our knowledge of Hell.

It was for love of Margarita (who gives her name to everything) that I began to write. I wrote every day, feverishly, from first light until the orders came to go out, to eat, to go to bed. Having Bevilacqua by my side accelerated the pace of my writing: I could confidently try out a line on him, or a chapter and, if it sounded as it ought, I set it down on paper. Bevilacqua was my rough draft. My text grew before my eyes. (Feverishly, confidently, as it ought, before my eyes: these words give me away. Every author discovers himself through his adverbs.)

I said that my feelings sharpen my intuition, they allow me to advance through the tunnels of the future, to see what my circumstances will or could be. I intuit, I guess (except that "guess" suggests improvisation) my destiny. Rubén is my canary in these cases. He senses before I do the lack of oxygen. His disgusting stench increases if there is a danger of asphyxiation, warning me to be prepared. And, of course, I make sure that I am.

Rubén was worried. His smell woke me up in the darkness; it had suddenly grown in intensity. Something was going to happen. Margarita tried to calm me down. During the nights on which they allowed her to stay (some libidinous jailer always came along to spy on us, like someone ogling two copulating beasts), she always begged me to be calm, telling me that they had said it would not be long until everything ended, and that they had assured her father that it wouldn't be long before I'd be free. But Rubén persisted. I must be prepared.

I slept as little and wrote as much as possible. By the time I reached the last word, I was exhausted.

Three hundred neatly filled pages. I picked up a plain sheet of paper and wrote the title on it, in capital letters. I was careful not to sign it. One of the many paradoxes of that place was that the few visitors were searched as thoroughly on leaving as they were on arrival, and it was strictly forbidden to take away letters or any material written by the detainees. Those being released, however – their number was even smaller – had the right to take out a bag or a suitcase, which was barely opened at the exit. I have seen (nothing in human nature surprises me now) a boy who had been badly tortured go home taking in his bag the small tweezers used by one of his torturers.

The following morning I said to Bevilacqua that if by chance he got out of this place before I did (I never wanted to contemplate the possibility of neither of us getting out), I would like him to take my manuscript with him. Surprised and, I think, touched, he promised me that he would.

Bevilacqua was what we once called – in those days before we lost our innocence – an "honest man". Did you know that, some time in the 1970s, in Argentina, the word "honest" began to acquire a connotation of "fool", of "dimwit"? I once heard a businessman use it contemptuously of some poor fellow he had tricked. *What can I say – he's an honest man!* It's strange how, during a dictatorship, words become infected by politics, lose their nobility and start to lie about themselves. The tongue is a sly little muscle, and goes wherever it likes. The nose, on the other hand, is like a loyal dog.

Rubén had warned me that something was up. When the guards came in to blindfold me, I knew that my faithful sniffer dog was not wrong. Then I heard a clear, deep and agreeable voice announce, in an expression of condolence it took me a while to understand, that Margarita would not be coming any more. The voice echoed in my head, as though I had received a blow. In schmaltzy, precise terms, the message was repeated. I understood what it was saying but, what infuriated me almost more than this extraordinary piece of news which threatened to destroy my world was the voice itself, sounding so polite, so cheerful and deliberate. *So this is it*, I told myself, *the impossible has come to pass. Margarita isn't here. Margarita is dead.*

An immense, cosmic fury overtook me. I realized that nothing that had happened to me up until that point had really mattered – neither the pain, the fear nor the lack of freedom. This voice was awakening me to my first, my only loss. I felt as though I had been broken in two, as if half of my body had been torn away.

I howled, I screeched, I vowed to do terrible things without knowing what they would be. The voice spoke in conciliatory tones, trying to provoke me, like someone putting out fire by throwing petrol on the flames. *Give us the number, and we'll let you see her one last time. Give us the second number, after all, it's no use to you any more, not with her in a pine coffin and you banged up between four walls. Give us the number and we'll let you out to see that she doesn't get slung into a pit, like a bitch.*

I tried to stand up and launched myself in the direction of the voice. A punch forced me down again. In the rush of blood to my bandaged eyes, I thought I saw Margarita among pinpricks of light; I saw her dissolve into something liquid and bright, and then I saw her no more. After that, several of them carried me to another cell and put me to sleep with a veterinary anaesthetic and a good kicking.

I don't remember the following months too well. Darkness, shouting, meals, some brief interrogation, more darkness... They had broken my glasses, so the half-light came as a relief, not as a hardship. Every now and then the voice spoke to me from the shadows. *Give us the number, and we'll take you to where she is, there is still time, the body takes a while to rot.*

One day several Cuban diplomats appeared in my cell, accompanied by a frowning general, and I left The Cesspit for ever. I arrived in Stockholm in the middle of a blizzard. It was the first time I had seen snow.

My lodgings were somewhere between a hospital and a convent. The sterile whiteness of the place exacerbated my physical problems and hurt my eyes. The Swedes gave me a new pair of dark glasses. In the mornings, a red-haired freckled nun brought me my breakfast, but I could find no reason to get up. Without Margarita, there was nothing. If I so much as shied a foot out of the blankets, I had the impression of falling into a void. Then I received a letter.

It's strange that no reader ever understood that my only subject is love. Or rather, I should say it *was* love, given that I shall never write again. Because it has taken me so many years to realize that she was enough, that she required no telling. Then time changed, thanks to her, who is in everything. Before, I had little faith, I said that things were impossible, that my world would vanish if I let it, like those faces we struggle to remember in a half-waking state. Now, with her letter in my hand, I didn't need even to breathe. She was alive: therefore everything continued to exist. Nothing was in doubt any longer. The mornings would no longer be a time of waiting for night, nor the night a postponement of the morning. The streets could once more be streets, not maps of meeting places, and the houses houses, not walls concealing an empty bedroom. She, who had always hovered on the edge of what was believable, had returned. She, without whom there would never have been any words, for the ink sprang from her veins, the paper was made from her skin. I was, am, the superfluous, unnecessary element. I am the grotesque redundancy.

Here I could give you one of those suspenseful pauses so beloved of spy films, but it would be intentionally bad literature. Margarita was in Spain. On her arrival at The Cesspit that evening, they had told her not to visit me again if she didn't want something horrible to happen to me; soon afterwards they advised her to leave the country. She managed to arrange for the Venezuelan Embassy to receive her in Madrid; there she had waited for months for news that never arrived. The voice had wanted to make me believe that I had lost everything, that there was no longer any reason for me to keep the code of the second account a secret – that, at any rate, the final chapter of my life had begun. Like Job's friend, the voice advised me: confess and die.

I read the letter, I got up, I filled in some forms, I asked them to take me to the airport, I arrived at Barajas that same night.

Margarita was working now at the Venezuelan Embassy in Madrid; it wasn't difficult for her to find me a job as a pen-pusher. I didn't mind what I did. I was with Margarita; I was out of prison. As I said before, I knew that I would never write again. I no longer felt that hunger, that thirst I had felt in the cell. As if to hush the echo of that infamous voice, I built my days in Madrid around Margarita's timetable and, when I found myself with her, a profound, immensely soothing calm enveloped me and wafted me to a placid sleep beneath a starry sky. I didn't need anything else. When you rediscover something so essential that you thought you had lost, that thing occupies all conceivable space. That's how it was with me.

That atmosphere of blessed torpor lasted a few months. No inner impulse, no outside spur tempted me. I lived purely in the present, far from everything, except Margarita. That was how I knew that no one in love ever writes. Because, I don't know if you'll agree with me, but writers are essentially disloyal, flitting from one passion to another; never dedicating themselves exclusively to one alone.

We were in Madrid, but we could have been anywhere. We went out for strolls, or we stayed in the flat that the Embassy had arranged for us: it was all the same to us. We went on the odd excursion, to Toledo, Alcalá de Henares, Chinchón: it didn't really matter. Everything happened now as though nothing else could happen, or had ever happened. There are insects that evolve from chrysalis to butterfly in a few hours and then die. That was how we lived. Then, one night, Margarita told me that she had seen Bevilacqua.

It was a sickening coincidence, a hideous shock. The truth is that we had forgotten about him, as we had forgotten about everything. Margarita had wanted to say hello to him, to tell him what had happened to me, to ask him how he was. But Bevilacqua had rushed away from her, like a hounded animal, and Margarita could not understand why.

That night when Margarita told me that she had seen him was like remembering a shipwreck. Hearing about Bevilacqua revived thoughts of my book, since my Robinson had perhaps – no, surely – been saved. Because, to be honest, I was so happy with Margarita that I hadn't spared a thought for *In Praise of Lying*. Now, suddenly, her encounter reminded me of those old pages. As though on a whim, I told Margarita that I wanted to get them back.

Cheerfully, we made plans, started thinking about the publication, the readers, the reviews, the recognition. I dared to imagine a new career, a new life, something to anchor us again in time and space. Table, paper, ink. Stories. Woven words.

We let a few days pass. Then, in one of the newspapers, we saw an ad for the launch of *In Praise of Lying*. Author: Alejandro Bevilacqua. My *Praise*. His book. Think about it. I felt abused, violated. I felt betrayed by a ventriloquist, a grey dampener, a real Drinkwater, as his name suggested.

"Let's go and see him," Margarita said.

We went to the launch. Not because I wanted to steal his thunder – do you understand? I don't care about all those prizes Argentine writers are always bragging about. One of my tropical compatriots, who never acquired the recognition he deserved until he was on the brink of death, claimed always to have lived "in a state of grace". I felt the same way. Given that I have been able to shoulder indifference with total dignity, some day, I told myself, I shall be totally indifferent to fame. If fame comes.

And I had Margarita.

But it poisoned my blood to see that crowd gathered at the behest of some puffed-up editor to celebrate, in the name of an impostor, the birth of something I had conceived. There they were: the scribblers, the poetasters, the key-bashers, the preening epistolarians. There they were: the babblers, the stammerers, the official cockatoos. All that brood who had once scorned me, pissing from a great height on my literary efforts – here they were now, applauding something they did not realize was mine. Margarita held my hand firmly, but it wasn't courage I was lacking now.

The bookseller-host had put out a few rows of seats. We sat down in the back row. When Bevilacqua took the stage, I fixed my eyes on him. Then he saw me. You know what happened next.

It was too late to reclaim my book, but I still needed to speak to Bevilacqua, to hear his explanations, which I already knew would not be credible. What did I want, then, you'll ask. I don't know if I ever really knew. To undo that other past, perhaps, to unravel the web of events, returning to the point at which I was dispossessed. At the end of the day, isn't that what we always want? Just because something is impossible, it doesn't stop us trying to attain it. Any traveller worth his salt wants to venture beyond the Pillars of Hercules.

Margarita found out that Bevilacqua had taken refuge at the home of that other Argentinian, the one who liked to pass himself off as French among Spaniards. We got past the doorman by pretending to have an appointment. Bevilacqua's face, when he opened the door, moved me – or almost moved me. From the back of the bookshop I had not realized how much my cellmate had aged.

Formalities come in useful at times like these. He invited us in; he offered us a seat; we sat down. He smiled. I smiled. Margarita smiled.

"My friend," began the lying thief. "You may not believe this, but I am happy to see you."

And then he told me what had happened.

Margarita and I listened with a patience that surprised us both. His departure from Buenos Aires, his arrival in Madrid, his meeting with the other exiles, his abduction by the Circean Andrea, the literary transformation of El Chancho into Bevilacqua.

"My friend, I never intended to take anything away from you. As for your manuscript, I think I may even have forgotten that I still had it. In making such a great effort to forget all that had happened in those years, I also lost something that deserved to be remembered. Don't blame me, I give you my word that I never meant to deceive anyone."

Misery does not easily provoke pity. On the contrary, a mangy dog invites you to throw stones. And yet I did feel sorry for Bevilacqua. There he was, my poor Judas, with his glory swiped away, grovelling for forgiveness like someone who's just pissed himself. My coat, which Bevilacqua had neglected to take, the central heating, which he evidently liked turned up, the muddle of this situation as disorientating as a mild nightmare, combined to make me feel awkward and uncomfortable. I asked if we could open the balcony windows.

Then the bell rang. Bevilacqua stood up and, motioning us to be quiet, left us alone in the sitting room. We heard some impassioned clucking, two or three words from Bevilacqua, and then nothing. After a few minutes, he came back to sit with us and, without saying who had visited, continued on his *excusatio*.

He spoke, without making much sense, about *In Praise of Lying* – not how I remembered my book, not how I knew it to be, but as though it were an ancient thing. It was as if he were talking about some very learned classic, so excellent as to render all commentary banal. He divested, not so much me, as himself of the book, telling me time and time again that it was not his work, that everyone would come to know that, that the author photograph adorning the back flap would be mine in all future editions.

Of course, you have never heard Bevilacqua speak, the way he made you lose yourself in a story. He was not a literary man. I mean that it was neither the feeling, nor the story behind his words that held his listeners' attention, but a kind of lulling plainsong in one key, rhythmic, uneven, *de la musique avant toute chose*. We had gone there to hold him to account, but he had turned the tables on us. He spoke as though relishing the words themselves. But he didn't smile; smiling was impossible for him. Whenever he made a stab at the gesture others might recognize as a smile, his face split in two, his nose dilated, his eyes creased as though he were focusing on his companion's jugular and his whole head, bony and greyish, tipped forward, not back, less like someone rejoicing than like someone getting ready to charge.

I'm not exaggerating: it was his serious rhetoric that seduced us. We had gone to see him because we wanted him to return what was mine; by the time he stopped talking, there was nothing left to return. *In Praise of Lying* belonged to nobody more than its readers; the Marcelino Olivares whose name would adorn future editions was simply another character in that kidnapped work; the supposedly piratical Bevilacqua was merely a miserable fraud, with no ship or ensign. Our unwittingly shared story had dissolved in a sea of confusion and misunderstandings. My thief had become a victim, like myself. And now, with the encouragement of Margarita, my Margarita, here I was consoling him.

The doorbell rang again, interrupting a moment ripe for pathos. Bevilacqua asked us again to be quiet, and again closed the door behind him, while we again strained to hear what was going on. Then, as though from a distant, half-forgotten place, I heard the voice, as always very precise, sirupy and kind. The voice wanted to know what had happened. Bevilacqua may have thought he had deceived everyone, it said, but he must understand that he had *not*. That the moment had come to speak clearly. That, without further excuses, he must tell him what we – Bevilacqua and your humble servant – were planning to do.

"I don't understand what you're saying," our poor friend replied, "but, if you want, you can ask him yourself." And he opened the door to the sitting room.

You never knew Gorostiza, and I don't know if anyone ever showed you a photograph of him. He looked like a Russian poet: a mane of hair that fell over one side of his face; a heavy black coat; always clutching a book in mutton-fisted peasant hands, although I don't think he was ever inclined to manual labour. I had been introduced to Quita, but never to him.

"Hello, Chancho," said the voice, dropping his bag containing the stolen bottles of sherry onto the floor. "And hello, Señora. I'm delighted to see you've come back from the dead."

"We were just leaving," Margarita answered and, gesturing to me, she went towards the door.

"Please stay, because this concerns us all. I was just asking our friend Bevilacqua how you were planning to share the Swiss funds."

"I don't know what you're talking about," said Bevilacqua.

"I'm talking about the funds, about money, about little bundles of green notes in a certain bank in Zurich. Ask your friend, who knows all about the subject – eh, Chancho?"

As if he owned the house, he strode to the balcony windows and closed them. In two bounds, Bevilacqua leapt across the room to open them again. Then, while these two squared up to one another, flapping the balcony door panels open and closed, I grasped the opportunity to take out my faithful bee and slip it into one of the bottles in Gorostiza's bag. As with books, *habeat sua fata apis.*

"Yes, we're going," I confirmed, taking Margarita by the arm.

Before closing the door, I turned round and managed to say to Bevilacqua that I congratulated him, that *In Praise of Lying* was magnificent. Downstairs, out on the street, I felt as though I were fighting for breath.

You'll understand why I haven't given you my postal address, esteemed Terradillos. Thanks to Margarita (and to Margarita's family, *semper fidelis*), El

Chancho has become a more discreet animal. Never mind the new name, new nationality, new disguise. Beneath the courtesies and formalities of a new nomenclature, I am still the caricature of that barrel-shaped boy who splashed around in the Camagüey mud.

Didn't I say that I believed in reincarnation? I am the proof. But I haven't been converted into an insect or a tree. No, I'm a Swiss gentleman now, in a three-piece suit, a camel-hair coat and a white silk scarf. My presence is so imposing that even Rubén is intimidated and rarely dares to make himself felt.

"Be honest and good, and you'll be happy," says the Blue Fairy to her puppet. It's a horrible lie, unless one is permitted to redefine *honest* and *good*. I think, in my case, both adjectives could apply. I have betrayed nobody but those who deserved betrayal, and I have been good to those on whom goodness is not wasted. This swine never scorned any pearls that were cast before him.

And Bevilacqua? I'm not so sure. In him, honesty got confused with ignorance, and goodness with sentimentality. It's not the same – we agree on that, don't we?

Bevilacqua was never happy, at least not after the disappearance of his woman, the only, true one. I was, possibly because Margarita was returned to me. In the sun, beside an impeccably blue lake, surrounded by perfectly ordered mountains, a thin shadow looms over my rotund body: it is her, the exclamation mark that complements my full stop, as her father once remarked, on seeing us together.

We are growing old. Yesterday, believe it or not, I had my seventieth birthday. My Margarita is a dozen years younger; even so, we can count the Januarys left to us. I miss my much-loved bee talisman, in which I once foolishly placed all hope of ultimate salvation. That is the price of revenge: the loss of something that could one day turn out to be indispensable.

We are growing old but, in truth, without bemoaning it much. Margarita not at all, and myself very little. There are things that I would still like to do, or that I would have liked to do differently, but that's how it is, and that's how it would always have been. During my first few years of financial exile, I received, through an intermediary, a communication from one Mendieta, retired police inspector, now presumably interviewing the Archangel Gabriel. Of course, I pretended not to heed it, but the nature of his questions revealed that this obscure and perspicacious Spaniard had guessed the truth. The thing is, we can never complete anything. Every artist knows that he is destined for imperfection.

I hope that these notes are useful for you, or at least that they help you in forming a picture of that skinny, ashen man who still wanders into my dreams from time to time. Then I can feel that his ghostly presence is shared. For a time, he unwittingly occupied my place in the universe. May he now occupy a place of his own. Let's not be small-minded, my esteemed Terradillos. Our molecules (our grandparents would say "our spirits") mingle and, in this vast cosmos of ours, it's impossible to know for sure to whom each particle, once belonging to a sun or star, now belongs.

I have the honour to remain, sir,

he who was, long ago and far away,
Marcelino Olivares

4

THE STUDY OF FEAR

If fondness moves you
To call yourself ingenious
For having found death for men where death was not,
To the study of fear we owe in turn
The design by which you lent a mere respite
To icy death from all its many blows.

Francisco de Quevedo
To the Inventor of the Artillery Gun

...nothing. I see nothing. I hear nothing. I feel nothing.
I advance through a thick fog, earth-coloured, like
dirty water. But I'm not even sure that this fog is
real. If I raise a hand (that is, if I believe myself to
be raising a hand), I cannot actually see it. If I try
to touch my face with my fingers, there is nothing
to let me know that I've achieved this aim. I can't
feel my fingers, I can't feel my face. At the moment,
for example, I believe myself to be speaking aloud,
but I can't make out any sound. I pull my hair, I
bite my tongue, I scratch my forehead: no pain,

no discomfort. I walk, I lie down, I sleep, I talk to myself, all the while sensing nothing. Nothing.

I thought someone asked me something.

Impossible. There are no voices here. There never were.

There are, and were. I don't even know what is happening to me. And what happened before.

Before what?

Before this nothingness. I thought that voice spoke again, the one I can't hear.

I carry on.

Backwards, sideways, in circles. It's all the same.

And always through this fog, the colour of dried blood.

Now I remember.

Something like this happened to me when, as a boy, I suddenly found myself in a sandstorm. Everything disappeared in a great cloud that stung my eyes, face and hands, choking the mouth and nose. One could not see, speak or hear. The world had become sand, and one feared becoming sand too. Then my father came out to look for me, pushing and shoving me back into the house. *Even the bitches know not to go outside when the wind gets up*, he said. I was always disappointing him.

Once, lost in a storm, I stumbled on some animal bones, gradually being polished by the sand. *I am going to end up like that*, I thought. Whitening bones, ever more transparent. And then, nothing.

I have a measured, smooth voice. I've been told that it's a lovely voice. My father, on the other hand, had a voice evoking something between thunder and barking.

My father's voice resounds, now, in my head. I don't hear it, in the silence that surrounds me, I don't hear anything, but I still have the impression of someone talking to me. It's a hoarse voice, malicious, sarcastic, accustomed to being obeyed. His military training lent him a certainty absent from other voices in my village, even the priest's. Our prestige depended on that voice.

I touch (but my fingers don't feel it) something metallic, something cold and embossed. His sabre's sheath. My skin remembers it.

The other boys showed off their lead toy soldiers, their bicycles. We showed my father's sabre, which we took down secretly in the dark sitting room among the furniture covered in dust sheets. Compared to his sabre, the security guard's machete was a mere penknife. This (my unfeeling hand slides over the surface, divested of weight and consistency) was our town's most precious emblem. *Colonel Gorostiza's sabre*, say the voices I cannot hear. *Has he ever cut a man's throat?* asks one. *He must have done, of course,* answers another. *They say that, under a special light, you can see the bloodstains on the blade.* At night, we children told each other, the blood on the sabre cries out in a very sharp, high-pitched shriek that only the bitches can hear.

My leg brushes against the shaggy coat of one of my father's bitches – all of them are a mix of German shepherd and Russian greyhound and of something else undefinable, like those great prehistoric wolves that I found once in a magazine. With the right hand that I can't see, I try to stroke one of them, but it is like stroking the wind. I call them: Annunciation! Visitation! Nativity! Presentation! Discovery! None of them replies.

My father was a mason and an ardent anticleric. He used to say that the notion of a god demanding constant praise filled him with contempt. *Your god needs more pampering than a French whore,* he lambasted the poor priest. *What sort of an Almighty can he be, if he needs people to tell him day and night: You're mighty! You're strong! You're awesome! What crap!*

My mother had tearfully begged him not to name his puppies after the Five Joyful Mysteries of the Rosary. He didn't deign to reply. My mother never dared to call them by these sacred names. Fearful of blaspheming, she would say, *here, here,* when she wanted them to come. Now I feel that it is her voice echoing mine.

Come along with us! bark the bitches through this cotton-wool air. They must be running the way they used to run then, in a long-haired pack, raising red dust. Only my father's voice restrained them.

My father liked to put on his uniform in the morning, the boots shining like ebony bowls, the belt pulled tight under his stomach, and then to go and sit at the door onto the street, drinking *maté*, the dogs sprawled at his feet. A smell of corn chowder filled the house (I am smelling it now), and my siblings and I, in starched smocks, took our leave of him with a brief reverence as we set off for school. The red dust clung to every part of us, even when there was no wind. But not to him, as though out of respect. Not even one grain dared to touch him.

As a young man, he had worked for an Irish landowner, who had wanted him to rid her land of Indians. A black plait, a memento of this work, hung in the dining room next to the sabre and a flag. Apparently, before I was born, a pair of Indian ears hung there too, but my mother refused to enter the house until he took them down. She had shown such uncharacteristic resolve in this matter that my father shrugged his shoulders and threw the ears out of the window. *The plait's staying*, was all he said.

The bitches keep howling. They want me to go with them; they demand it with their shrill yapping. Within this dream (which isn't mine), I sense them run towards something that they are going to tear to shreds. When they were lying at my father's feet (he would stroke their bellies with one hand, while the other held on to the maté) I used to look at their terrible teeth, exposed by the black lips, and imagine them sinking into flesh, grinding bones. The bitches' soft, brown eyes gazed at my father. *How can they belong to the same face, those eyes and those teeth?* I wondered. Then my father smiled, his brow softened and a gold tooth showed between his lips, beneath the moustache.

The owner of my nightmare shivers.

Now I know that the bitches have reached their prize. They're not my bitches any more, or rather they are, but they are also different, wilder, with enormous alabaster fangs. I can see them now, on the other side of a vast dump, pouncing on a boy who falls face down in the filth. Someone shouts at them to stop, but it's too late. The boy tries to stand up, his shirt is torn to shreds, part of his left cheek is missing. *For fuck's sake!* says the colonel (another one, not my father — this happens years later, I'm a man now). *Let's see if next time someone can control these animals!* A group of soldiers scares the hounds away. *Next time*, an echo repeats in my head, across the unfathomable depths of time. That experience at the dump ought to have taught me something. Perhaps I would have been able to endure all this better.

I advance.

There are things one doesn't learn from, only remembers.

Who's asking me something? What does she want?

What, stuck in the house again? You're going to make yourself ill, Titito, with so much reading. Let me bring you a better light. My mother comes and goes, anxious. I read everything: the poems of Capdevila. *Billiken*. The Sopena dictionary. *An Expedition to the Ranquel Indians*. My mother always looks worried. She has my brothers and sisters to look after. There are seven of us. No, eight. Santiago was born so much later than the rest of us that we forget to count him. My father never mentions him.

My father was clear about hierarchies. *Friends first, then country, and family last of all*, he would say. And to us: *pissing and making you lot – it all came out of the same hole.*

My mother's voice is joined by my father's. *Tell that poofter son of yours that I don't want to see him indoors until the afternoon. He can go where he likes so long as it's out in the sun.* The sun only shines for a few hours during these winter months. I take the opportunity to practise the poems I've written, but find myself reciting others, the ones I know by heart, thanks to the books that Señorita Amalia, my teacher, lends me. Joaquín V. González, Rubén Darío, Espronceda. *"Sail on, sailing boat, without fear."* *That "without fear" implies that he is, in fact, afraid,* I write in my notebook. I'm learning to read poetry.

But writing's shit. My father always knew that, and I didn't believe him.

A brief bio-bibliographic interlude. I studied Literature in Río Gallegos, I enrolled on a course on European Literature, but it was useless – one boring class after another. I tried to make friends with other students. *Yes, me too! Of course – where do I sign? United we stand, unto victory or death.* We'd protest against any old thing, demanding our right to be heard. *Never a step backwards. (But to what end? I asked myself, though I did not dare say so aloud).* And at night I wrote. *Let me sing of my land, things I imagined I loved.* But now I was composing jingles. Exalting armed combat, against enemy tigers. Songs, hymns, marches. Before leaving for Buenos Aires, I published a little book at the local press. I paid for the printing myself. A thousand copies. *Red March.*

My childhood as I wanted it to be, and a eulogy to the revolution that I had never seen and which mattered little to me. The owner of the press, an anarchist from Asturias, gave me a hug and a discount. *Poetry is also politics*, he told me, *of the best and strongest kind.* I took away my books wrapped up in brown paper and secured with twine. In Buenos Aires I left little piles of them in bookshops, when no one was looking. Thieving, in reverse. Then I started working at an insurance company.

I confess that I never had a single reader, let alone a review. The world failed to register the presence, the existence, of my verses. One day I saw, at the entrance to a bookshop, beside the discarded cardboard and packaging, half a dozen copies of my book waiting for the rubbish collectors. I gave them a wide berth as I passed, denying them, like a traitor. *Never again,* I told myself, *never again. I made a mistake. I dared to do something improper.* How could I have been so presumptuous as to think I might be read? I kept a few copies at the back of my wardrobe, like someone hoarding the pornographic magazines of his adolesence.

I stop.

In this fog, names keep coming at me. Of the places where I've worked. Of the places where I've lived. Of friends who have died. Of half-read books. Of anonymous faces. Of cities that I do not remember having visited. Of train stations. Of publicity posters. Like a great invisible parade of names, a mob of fanatics brandishing flags. Colonia Mariana. Gerstein Insurance Company. Elsa. Villa Plácida. *Songs of Life and Hope*. School friends. Juan Ignacio Santander. Ovidio Goldenberg. Boedo. Ostrovsky's *How the Steel Was Tempered*. Cela Mondacelli. El Sordo. *El Cronista Comercial*. Los Gatos restaurant in Madrid. Blanca. Goytisolo's *Campos de Níjar*. Bilbao.

The letters dance around, dissolve, coalesce. I am overwhelmed by a cacophony of words I don't understand. More barking.

Who's calling me?

I wish I could tear off this unfeeling skin in order to feel again.

I move forward.

Anyone who has ever set words down on a page never loses the habit of writing, even when not writing. The calligraphy persists, like an army of ants that can't be stopped. Behind closed eyelids, the words gather, call one another, pair off. An anthill of letters bursts forth and pursues me, black and red batallions which attack one another, get mixed up in the sand, climb up the bitches' legs, burrowing into their fur. They bite, advance, devour. The bitches howl. A dictionary has launched itself into this inconceivable space in which I am walking.

Visitation. Presentation. La Perla. Don Felipe Pereira. Colonel Aníbal Chartier. Carrasco. *Consider the lilies of the field*. Liliana Fresno. La Resistente. Señorita Amalia. Cáceres. Hendaya. Belem and Sons. Angélica Feierstein. Quilmes Beer.

That's enough.

After I started working at the insurance company, I never wrote again, or scarcely.

Only once, years later, reading that long-forgotten writer Manuel J. Castilla in an anthology that was prohibited at the time, did I once more feel the urge to make something out of words. Castilla had written:

> He who goes through the dead house,
> and who along the corridor at night
> remembers the afternoon of leaden rain
> as he pushes open the heavy door.

But no, it was impossible now.

Before, as an adolescent, everything moved me. The flat landscapes of my village. The red hills on the horizon. Winter and the feeling of cold in poor people's houses. The misery of those who worked on the large plantations. The suffering of others, which I tried to imagine as my own. To sing of the mason's hands, of the widow's eyes, of Tolstoy's and Ciro Alegría's redeemed heroes. To be their poet.

But no, you fool. You should never have tried it. I still feel ashamed of it.

I told myself never to try again, although, at night, in half-waking moments, I would still string words together to the rhythm of certain melodies. What would the Colonel have thought, I wonder, of that double treachery, writing instead of doing, talking instead of writing? It disgusted him that any son of his should be a poet rather than a soldier, but also that I should not have continued in the career that I myself had chosen. It would surely have disgusted him even more to know of my Judas vocation for, although he did not believe in Christ, he still regarded him as a good lad, albeit a bit off the rails. *Doubtless it was the father who convinced him that he was a god; in my view a stint in the Roman army would have done him a world of good.*

I advance like an intruder in someone else's garden, at night, in the dark, feeling my way. I imagine the owner of this garden, in the distance, at the mercy of this troubling nightmare, my suffering dreamer. *It's me*, I want to tell him, *don't be scared, whoever you are. It's only me, whoever I am. Keep sleeping, I won't hurt you, I won't do anything, good or bad. I only want to talk to you, just talk.*

Somniloquist: one who talks in his sleep (*Sopena's New Illustrated Spanish Dictionary*).

Even after I stopped writing, I continued to read the dictionarly feverishly. A present from my mother. Parallelepiped. Paremiology (which means the study of proverbs). Prosaic. Prostate. Prostitution. The words flit past, daring me to catch one. Presbytery. Presidence. Prodigious. Profound. Progeny.

I don't want to do this. That linguistic cosmography is no longer anything to do with me. I wish I could lock all those philological abortions up in a great library and set fire to it. Reduce the universe to illiterate ashes. Find something else to occupy me.

Over the white skeletons of the slaughtered dogs run words which I no longer try to follow with my eyes. Let's allow them to keep running, with their thousand feet, their fibrous wings, their antennae probing the air: there is nothing left to eat. Once, on that dump, I picked up the skull of a boy who had been thrown into a lime pit. Don't ask how. The colonel doesn't like to be asked questions. An adolescent's skull is the same size as an old man's. Like an imbecile, I said to myself: *And what about experience, accumulated memories? How do they fit into a little box like that?* Mark this, Master of my nightmare: I once had feelings.

Now I understand more. Now that I have no flesh or bones, I believe that none of that is contained: it comes in and goes out through pores in the rock, like a stream, like air, like this constant cloud of sand, no beginning or end.

First recollection or last memory. Who knows. It's impossible to be sure.

Let's count them. One, two, three, twenty-five, six hundred thousand memories.

The army of letters is joined now by figures. An alphabet of numbers.

Everything is in code.

I feel exhausted.

I know that the true invasion has yet to begin.

Perhaps it will never begin.

The nights before are always the most frightening.

I carry on. I continue.

A writer denounces reality as he sees it.

Imagination filters it.

Inspiration feeds it.

But he has to know when to stop.

To know when what is written is shameful, as I knew my writing to be.

Not this.

Throw it out.

Scratch it out, tear it up.

Then, what remains?

I don't mean this as an excuse, let me make that clear. To give another use to the words. To tell what others do. Because every chronicle is also a file.

My father used to say that the army's strength is in its secrets. Yes, Colonel, sir. I'll tell you about it. This is what I saw. This is what I heard. Tom said this to Dick. Harry's lying: I heard him saying this thing and that thing. The difference between gossip and betrayal is the seriousness with which one operates. A gossipmonger writes novels; I drafted reports. Which is the more honorable craft?

Onwards.

Buenos Aires devours everything. For a poor boy from the south, it was like a giant chessboard, with massive, granite pieces, full of sinister nooks, obscene crannies. I went there. I took a room on the third floor of a house on Calle Alsina, friendly landlady, doling out *maté* and cake. In the neighbouring rooms, young couples from the north, El Chaco and Córdoba, bank employees, two single sisters. In the morning, at lunchtime and in the evening, the *barrio* filled with youngsters on their way to and from school. At thirty-something, I'm old now and working for Belem Importers. Now and then, I jot down some verse I've composed, to rid myself of it, to get it off my chest.

I was solitary. Anyone who's had too many brothers and sisters quickly gets used to having none. It was easy, at that time, to put on masks. Nothing had any substance, nothing seemed real. Not even our merchandise, not even the bread or the wine. In the shops no one bothered putting price tags on anything any more. *This morning it cost ten thousand pesos, this afternoon fifteen thousand.* You had to spend your monthly salary in the first week, or lose half its worth.

I receive a letter from my father. *Things are hard. If you need work, go and see my friend, Colonel Chartier, my brother-in-arms. I'll let him know you'll be going to see him. Look your best, get a haircut.*

It's true that I didn't know how much longer I would last in that job. What job? *Keep putting on zeros – nothing really has a price any more.* It was impossible to import anything, or to export anything either. *It's not even worth sending them a bill: translate it into dollars and you'll see that we're the debtors here.* Señor Belem's children moved to São Paulo. *I'll close the shop the day I die*, said the old Belem, as wrinkled as a prune. *You've got a job here until then.* My mother, meanwhile, a prisoner of her own misery, wrote to tell me that nothing at home had changed.

Now I'm struggling to breathe. The invisible sand enters my mouth and nose, filling my lungs, transforming itself. Sand into air, air into blood, blood into mud. Everything is dragging me back. I'm at the beginning again. In fog again, and darkness. Once more, I advance.

That's how it was.

One afternoon, coming out of the Lorraine cinema, I bumped into a girl with straight, black hair, a smooth brow, very white. We started talking about something or other and she invited me to go for a drink. I've never found it easy dealing with women. I can still hear my father's advice: *The world is divided like this: first, dogs; second, comrades; third, friends; fourth, personal stuff; fifth, women.*

I saw out my adolescence as a virgin. My first encounter was at twenty, with the older sister of a classmate, in Río Gallegos. Liliana Fresno. One night, waiting for my friend on the sofa of their house, Liliana started playing around with me. She sat down beside me, unbuttoned my shirt, then took me to her room. I thought: there it is, that's it, that's enough.

At the insurance company there was a girl, Mirta, who used to smile at me. I wrote her a poem. One afternoon, I saw that she and her friends were laughing and looking at me. I realized that I had been foolish, that my verses had amused her. I didn't speak to her any more after that. I saw her, years later, in Buenos Aires. I pretended not to recognize her.

The girl at the Lorraine laughed a lot, but she didn't mock me. She would have seen me, I suppose, as an older man, given that she was twenty-eight and I was thirty-five. In those days, thirty-five was a considerable age. Now, I could be twice as old and still be younger than I was then.

The girl asked me what I was reading. I was carrying the banned anthology in my pocket. I showed it to her. She laughed again. *Go on, read me something*. I don't remember what I read her, but I was pleased to let her hear my voice, watching her furtively as my eyes followed the verses on the page. *I'd like you to read to me in bed*. I looked at her as if I had not understood. *I'd like to go to sleep with you reading to me*. I paid for the coffees and we left.

Now, in the red mist, I bump into great sheets of paper which are hanging in the wind, as though from a washing line. Dry, rough paper, of the type used in books published by Austral, which absorbed the ink so badly. They don't tear as I advance, they are impervious to my weight: only light and time age them. It's not that I feel them (I feel nothing), but I know that they are hanging here, as though to obstruct my path. Something is printed on them, but

I don't know what. I see nothing, hear nothing.

I don't like reading, her voice says to me, *but I like being read to. Any old thing. Even the phone book, if you want. I like watching your lips move, I like the colour of your tongue.*

More names. More words. More verses by Castilla.

> I am growing from you
> I am a new leaf, barely touched by the breeze,
> I am that summer...

I can make out letters on the sheets as though on a blurred letter chart at the optician's. I recite with the book open on the bed, the girl beside me, caressing her own breasts to the rhythm of my voice.

> I am that summer that feels its breast
> heavy with fruits
> and which falls upon you, making you fertile.

Somehow I kept on reading, and later I asked if I could see her again. *I'm with someone,* she said. *But we'll probably run into each other again.* And she handed over my clothes.

I don't know if it's different for someone who's used to surprises. But for me, whose life had until then been a predictable series of more or less sensible events, to fall in love was an intrusion of the impossible. Until then, I could explain everything. Every fact had its cause, every decision its consequence. My world was logical and coherent, as formal as a sonnet, or at least my sonnets, in which the final verse contrived to be surprising, and therefore never was. "Here it comes," my quartets announced. "Any minute now," predicted the first tercet. And so it was. Laws of gravity and dynamics ruled my world, inside and out. She was my first encounter with the inexplicable.

During those months, I repeatedly went to the Lorraine, hoping to find her. One day I saw her, on the arm of a very thin, smiling man. I don't know if she saw me. I realize that, with the exception of those few hours we spent together, I was invisible to her. I, on the other hand, never lost sight of her. I remembered her every night; I knew every corner of her body and imagined expeditions across her increasingly familiar geography. That was then. Now, I wouldn't even be able to say what colour her eyes were.

After work, I liked to explore the bookshops on Calle Corrientes. I looked for old poetry books in battered editions, by long-dead authors. I bought them for myself, to make me feel less alone, but also in order to read them to her.

One day, while I was riffling through the tables in one of those bookshops, two men ran in and carried off a young man who, minutes before, had been reading at my side. As they bundled him into the car, I heard someone call me: *Hey, you with the long hair, aren't you Colonel Gorostiza's son?* A man in a double-breasted suit and dark glasses placed his hand on my shoulder. *Your father wrote to me saying you'd be calling. How about it?* He smiled, handed me a card and walked off up the street. I carried on looking for a book.

Seeing her and hearing her mattered to me less than touching her. Skin is a space that stands in for the world. When we touch it, brush against it, it encompasses everything. Now I move forwards through the fog, but then my fingers moved over her valleys and hills like determined pilgrims, barely resting, retracing their steps sometimes to try another route, exploring unknown pathways. Now that all touching is forbidden me, that landscape of skin sinks under my weight, envelops and stifles me. I tumble into a sack that closes over me, damp and spongey, made of my own flesh. My fingers want to climb the slopes of that body, but the slopes keep getting steeper. It's impossible to get a grip. The skin, warm and sticky now, encloses me and my cloud of clay-like dust. The air turns to mud, filling my eyes, mouth and nostrils. The mud turns to water. I'm drowning. My throat burns. The water turns to air. Then the panic abates. I breathe.

Again.

Every memory, this whole suffocating multitude of memories, leads to nightmares. Here there is nothing more than that, things that I believe once happened. Forgive me, my dreamer, for infecting you with so much horrible stuff. It isn't wilful – I can't try to do anything. Every time I attempt to retrieve an instant of joy, a moment in which I was happy to live, a black stain spreads over it, obliterating everything. Her in the damp sheets, her panting on the pillow, her digging furrows in my back with her nails, her, too, turning into that fathomless mud in which I am forever sinking. And I rise up again. And I sink in again.

I cannot even salvage that first moment of memory. Nothing clean, nothing happy, nothing that does not grow dark.

Darkness is also Buenos Aires. I've never known such a murky city, with those streets which branch off from an illuminated avenue to lose themselves among secret trees and unsuspected sturdy walls, abrasive to the touch. Here, at least at the start of those years, darkness is not frightening. I follow the instructions in her note, which is unsigned, but written in the tidy handwriting of a model pupil. *Come to see me tomorrow at eleven. Ring twice and I'll open the door.* I obey. I arrive, I ring the bell, the barred gate opens, I go up some steps, I push open the door. She hasn't put the light on, but I can see my way. There's a smell of summer, of apricots, of rain. A hand takes mine and pulls me onto a mattress. I fall, I sink, but I'm not drowning. I breathe deeply. We say nothing to one another.

I like talking to you alone, mouth to mouth.
Telling you all the things you don't want to say.

In love, there is one condition that is more terrible than the others. Overwhelming, exclusive, jealous, blind to all reason. Its language is coarse, brutal, abusive. Its gestures are sometimes gentle, at other times of a terrifying violence. It never speaks the truth, because it fears itself. And it lies to keep people from believing all the things that it is. It consists almost entirely in an imagined body: enormous hands, enormous eyes, enormous tongue, gigantic sex. Its limbs have atrophied, grown so small as almost to disappear. The lover has no legs or chin. The nose appears and disappears, as do the ears. A breath, a moan conjure them, and then they vanish again. In that amorous reality there are more bloodthirsty armies than the ones commanded by my father, packs of hounds more rabid than the five bitches in my worst nightmares. You may complain now, dreamer, of the nightmares I foist onto you. Thank your stars that you have been spared this other one.

I recognize this sense of suffocation that I'm feeling now, this sinking into mud. I was here before, but it was worse then, when my flesh still existed and my brain was working. Worse was the fear of hearing (and of not hearing any more) the desired answer to the question. *When shall I see you again?* She looks at me with those amused eyes and says that she doesn't know, and I'm not to worry – enjoy the moment.

To live in the present: the definition of hell.

I leave, with her perfume clinging to my clothes. I don't shower. In the office, on the bus, beneath the blanket, at night, I imagine that she is there. I can think of nothing else. I walk aimlessly. I eat, in no particular restaurant, boiled food, on starched tablecloths. I flick through books which I have no intention of reading. I go to the Lorraine, but don't watch the film. On the contrary, I can't wait for it to end, so that I can go and stand at the entrance and look for her among the women who come out chatting with their boyfriends, or alone, or in gaggles of shrieking friends. She isn't there, of course. I return to the darkness of my street and fumble for the lock. I grow experienced in unlocking doors in the dark.

My mind repeats: she, she, she, she. *Ella, ella, ella ella.* I try to hush it, but it's impossible. Two graceful volutes culminating in infinitely drawn-out lines. The city is full of inverted Ionic columns, like the extended façade of a Greek temple upside down. Everything is *ella*.

Don Belem dies. One of the sons returns from Brazil to close the business down. He offers me a job in São Paulo, but how can I go so far away from her? The man doesn't understand, and thinks I'm ungrateful. When saying goodbye to the other employees, he leaves me out. Returning home, I walk past the Military Circle, and remember that this is where Colonel Chartier has his office. I go in and ask for him. A corporal takes my documents and leads me to an office dominated by a gigantic desk and a gold-framed mirror. The ceiling is adorned with cherubs.

Inside the placenta bag in which I am sinking, something (a knife, a sabre, a claw) has torn at the walls and is dragging me out, on a viscous and foul-smelling wave. One Roman torture consisted in making a prisoner drink wine, then thrusting a knife into his stomach. Like the wine in that Roman's stomach, I'm dragged along by a river I can't see.

I spin around several times. I hear nothing, feel nothing. I hit the bottom.

In the watery gloom, I make out three tall, military figures, their chests covered in phosphorescent medals. The first has no face, only an immense arc of sharpened teeth, through which protrudes a fat, purple tongue. The second is a tangle of hair, as rough as steel wool, as sharp as barbed wire. The third has the features of Colonel Chartier, well-shaven cheeks, a neat black moustache, dark glasses, a military peaked cap. In front of them are dozens of little naked people, raising their arms before this terrible triumvirate. Then the teeth begin to chew on the tongue, the tangle of hair bursts into flames, and Colonel Chartier's face breaks up, handfuls of worms pushing their way through the cracks. In unison, the triumvirate utters a howl and vanishes. In the darkness, some whitish, rough-edged residue remains, like phlegm.

Colonel Chartier steps out from behind the desk and takes my hand. My father has spoken of me to him. *How is my old friend? Lumbago troubles all of us. But what do you youngsters know of that! Life seems eternal to you. How old are you? Forty-one already? I don't believe it! Can you manage a coffee? Now then, corporal, bring us two coffees. Well, well. Where were we?* And he offered me a job.

I never enquired as to the official name of the department led by Chartier. We called it COM-MUNICATION, and the folders were marked with a capital C and a serial number. A secretary, practically a teenager, had the job of filing them. I never knew who used them, nor when, nor why.

Colonel Chartier declares: *As for you, all you have to do is pay attention. Your father told me that you have a special talent for that. "He has a bloodhound's sense of smell," my friend Gorostiza said. And that's what we need here. People who know how to sniff the air, to catch things most people miss. These are treacherous times, my young friend. Anything could be a trap. The enemy looks just like you or me, and no sooner we're distracted than we'll have a knife at our throats. Civilization and Barbarism. I don't need to ask which side you're on.*

My job entailed presenting myself in his office at eight o'clock in the morning to receive my instructions. After coffee with a dash of milk (it was never served black in Colonel Chartier's office), my six or seven colleagues and I, all men, would be handed a folder (C27658, C89711) with an address, a time, sometimes a name. I spent innumerable days sitting in a particular bar close to Congress or standing on the platform of the Pacífico station, waiting for something to happen, for someone to arrive.

In one pocket I carried a little book of poems, to while away the time; in the other, the identification badge they had given me, with the naval crest in embossed tin, which felt like my father's sabre. Sitting in the bar, or standing at the station, I held the book from which I read in one hand, while the other rubbed the crest, warming it with my fingers. At the end of the day, I would return to the office for a debriefing. Occasionally, I had to go out at night.

Whenever I saw what I had been sent to see, I gave a signal with my hand, and the agents got on with their work. I learnt not to recognize them; it was they who looked out for me. Nor did I want to know anything about the people I was spying on. Their variety surprised me. It was impossible to generalize. There were all sorts. Gentlemen in overcoats. Workers. Pensioners with the newspaper tucked under their arms. Mulattos. Old ladies with blue rinses. Teenagers with acne. Young men who must have been university students or who worked, as I had done, in some anonymous insurance company. Ditto young women. The odd priest. The odd nurse. The occasional secondary-school teacher.

Once I was sent to spy on an ex-colleague, a woman of about forty who had worked in Accounts at Belem Exporters – Chela something-or-other. I had scarcely noticed her when we were working in the firm. Reserved, well turned out, invariably in very high heels, she was, someone told me, a widow with two children. Now she appeared very agitated, her hair dishevelled. She was carrying a briefcase which she kept opening and closing. As she got off the train, I immediately recognized her, and motioned with my hand. I think that she saw me and thought that I was waving to her. When the agents closed in on her, she shouted and started to run, but then one of her heels broke, and she almost fell onto the tracks. She looked up at me, or at least in my direction, as she sprawled on the ground. I left before they took her away.

Thick and sticky filaments of phlegm cling to my body, hindering my movements. Its tentacles almost seem to have a life of their own, the way they roam over my arms and legs, my neck and face. It's like being clasped to the bosom of a jellyfish, like growing another layer, slimy and warm, over my own skin. It's as though I've been turned inside out, my organs exposed, my guts intertwined with this fibrous filth. They tighten my throat, strangling me with gelatinous fingers, finding new methods of suffocation. The filaments probe my nose and mouth, filling my lungs to the point of bursting. And once more, all around me, the dust cloud. The phlegm has disappeared. I move forward in a space I cannot see.

If I could stop thinking, even for a moment, I could rest, regain strength. If I could cease, for a moment, vomiting this string of images, of words, of things past.

I try to focus on a dark point, on a pinprick of nothingness. Impossible. The point expands, fills with twinkling lights, each light something lived, something remembered. And I go back to the beginning. My parents' house. The bitches. My siblings. The poems. The city at night. My elusive lover. Blood and broken bones. My reports. Her. *Ella.*

Sometimes I inform on boys and girls who are really very young. *It's a way of protecting them,* Colonel Chartier tells me. *It's our duty as fathers of the nation.*

I see them gathering outside the school gates (I still live in the little room on Calle Alsina), and I stand close to the newsstand, pretending to be choosing sweets, watching them. It occurs to me that I am rather like a satyr, hidden in the undergrowth, spying on nymphs. Or like the elders devouring Susanna with their eyes, nostalgic for their erections. Or like some depraved pornographer, flashing open his dirty mac in the playground.

I watch and make notes. Sometimes I can hear them. They tell each other nonsense, lark about, inventing a rhetorical world and a new golden age.

Demonstrations, petitions, declarations, a whole vocabulary of banner-waving and end-of-year speeches. I was fifteen once too.

I make my lists. I question the doorman, perhaps a waiter, the uniformed police officer who barely understands what I am asking him. And then I hand in my homework on time – I'm never late. *You and punctuality are like twin brothers*, says the Colonel.

And we go back to the start.

Every so often, at unpredictable and over-lengthy intervals, I would see her. We met almost by chance; I would receive a note proposing a date, or I would be bold enough to call her at work, in some faculty office. One day, I left my book for her, beside the bed. I never knew if she had read it. I didn't dare ask her. It was enough to know that it was there, at her side. It meant that I was there too, my words on her lips, my tongue in her mouth.

I can see that my story is exciting you, my dreamer. It's making your blood flow faster, prompting you to delve into your own memory in search of amorous memories. I warn you: don't follow me. My hunting grounds are dangerous. All of them begin as tended gardens which sprout suddenly into jungles, into minefields, into quicksand. You won't reach the other side.

Two simultaneous events changed everything.

There is a first moment (we don't realize it's the first) when we cross the threshold of a forbidden room, somewhere we ought never to enter. We do it without thinking. A key accidentally placed in the wrong lock, the door unintentionally opened, the splashes of blood on the floor that we ought not to have seen – just like in fairy tales.

Two events: her telling me, as we woke up, *I can't see you again. Not any more.* And then that morning, on the letter of instructions, her name heading a new list of quarries.

She doesn't want to see me any more, because she wants to see the other man. I say "other" because I am not unique. I am one of two, one among many. I want to know who my rival is. Who has privileges over her. Who is this person causing my dismissal from her presence. *You don't know him. What does it matter to you?* And she smiles. I grab her hair. I yell at her to answer me. She refuses. I shout louder. I shake her, I yank her hair harder, as though to tear it from the fearful, distant face looking back at me. I slap her. She utters a name. *What?* She repeats it. *Say it again.* She says it again, crying. My open hand is still hitting her. And now, for sure, I've crossed to the other side and the door is closing behind me.

There is a condition of love more terrible than the others: I repeat this like a litany. It is almost the sum of my learning. I can't help it. Sometimes it remains latent, like a snake, sleeping beneath the sheets. More often it bursts into flames, like a salamander, consumed by its own heat. I know this monster down to the last detail. It has three heads and a triple, avenging shadow. I could not stop it even if I wanted to. And I don't want to. I want everything to burn. Her, especially, silently screaming.

> I like talking to you alone, mouth to mouth.
> Telling you all the things you don't want to say.

The name she mentioned is not on the list. I pick up my pen and add it, clearly writing it beside hers. I go home, shower, dress, set off for work. At midday, I position myself at the door to Casa Gold, where the rings in the shop window announce engagements and anniversaries, silver and gold weddings. I am no longer a disinterested professional, spying for other people. What I'm doing now is personal – private business. *How is it possible to be betrayed like this?* I ask, as people come and go, rarely bumping into each other, borne along on sinuous currents that hardly touch each other. The vision of the multitude dissolves. Images of her are superimposed onto others, this time of butchery, of dismembered bodies, Bluebeard's brides with bloodied stumps and stomachs cut open. *Let everything end, so that she will end*, I say to myself. And I am still waiting.

Various people begin to assemble. I don't know why they are demonstrating. Nor do I want to know. I don't read the banners, I don't listen to the chants. I don't see her in the growing crowd, either, but I know she's there – I can smell her. And doubtless him, too. A common cause. Both of them guilty. Both of them condemned. The surge of people hides them, but does not protect them. If I stretch out a hand, I can touch them.

The crowd begins to walk along Diagonal towards the Plaza de Mayo. On the pavements, spectators. At the end, the mounted police, their sabres still sheathed. I walk along among the onlookers, with an absent expression. Outside the Boston Bank, I spot Chartier's agents, unmistakeable now. I make a slight gesture, and they join the procession.

When the marchers reach the Plaza de Mayo, the mounted police charge, as planned. Then I see her, shining in the dark crowd. I look for the agents, but they have disappeared in a mêlée of legs, sabres, people's heads and horses' heads. The clamour is deafening. Clouds of tear gas explode on the pavement opposite. The crowd is herded towards Calle Florida. Then I suddenly see her, leading the thin man by the arm. He's covering his face with his hand, and his face is covered in blood. And she is tending to him.

Dust, fog, mud, water, dense, indeterminate moods, fathomless, formless seas, a world suspended between solid and liquid, viscosities, globules of spit, blood. Myself, trapped for ever; her, forever cleaning his wound, diluting his blood in water, an obscene and economical eucharist. My state condemns me to this vision, it's a professional obligation, an occupational hazard. But I don't resign myself to it. This is also torture.

I see the agents, and point out the couple to them, sitting in a café window emblazoned with the words "Cerveza Quilmes". Take away the noise, gunfire, screaming, the smoke, the people running, the water, the blood, the agitated waiter – and what's left? Two lovers at a café, hand in hand, one head bowed towards the other, a man and his sweetheart.

How dare she exclude me? That paradise is mine. I see her stand up to go; he stays behind. I signal to the agents to follow her. We'll see about him later. She (I run through the practical exercises that Chartier insists are essential) will suffer all the interrogations, all the punishments, all the deaths. One alone is not enough for me.

I don't know where they took her. I never wanted to know it, because I preferred to imagine the whole lot. I never tried to find anything out, even though everything is recorded in the folders (C56908, C99812), every raid, every prisoner, every building, every procedure, every conclusion. *This has to be run like a bank,* says Colonel Chartier. *We should be able to account for every last centavo.*

Weeks went by, months. I moved, within the same department, from informing to gathering information. The first job entailed observing. The second required questions. A friend of my father, an amateur botanist, used to claim that all he did was to classify, in great ledgers, whatever he happened to find in nature; he left the whys and wherefores to academic luminaries. I, on the other hand, did not regard the move from lookout to inquisitor as a step up. It was simply another aspect of the same job – using the tongue instead of the eyes. *Now you can give your eyes a rest,* joked the Colonel.

One can get used to anything (except for this, except for what comes after, except for nothingness). One gets used to the sight of a person deprived of all hope, to tears, to screams, to deliberately inflicted wounds, to vomiting and blood, to picturing another's pain as though it were being drawn for you with coloured chalks. The hours go by, and afterwards one forgets, or pretends to forget. One has to make an effort not to forget.

I remember.

There he was, calmly walking down the street, he who had hijacked her affections, robbed me of her skin, trespassed on my territory. There he was, poor bastard, oblivious to my existence. For the sake of my own honour, I had to convince myself and convince the others that he was not merely a fool, a nonentity in the enemy army, but on the contrary, a glorious captain, a paladin, someone we must use all our cunning and might to overthrow. After his hell, his purgatory. I was generous enough to allow him a new life in Europe, a way to prolong my pleasure in dreaming of his end. No one ever extended such consideration to me.

I would venture to say that I worked well. Without the distraction of feelings or literature, I threw myself entirely into my duty. *Noblesse oblige.*

I'm invited to an official ceremony at the Military Circle – I no longer recall in whose honour – a party with medals and sabres beneath crystal chandeliers and the inevitable gilded mouldings. Colonel Chartier makes a speech; others follow. Applause. In the room sit various rows of decorated military men and their wives. An enormous, mountain-shaped woman occupies one or more seats in the front row, her blue silk dress spread over her stomach like a giant sail, at the stern of a swell of uniforms. After the ceremony, the Colonel introduces me to a little man with a moustache and bushy eyebrows. *General, this is the boy I told you about. Colonel Gorostiza's son.* The little man looks me up and down and says nothing.

Somebody must have appreciated my efforts, because the Colonel calls me to his office one Sunday, soon after the party. *Do you go to Mass? No? Quite right; church is for sissies. I'm going to give you some good news, you deserve it.* And he announces that the General (the most recent one) wants to send me to Spain. *A new broom,* says the Colonel. *But I think the changes are good. All that scum we've been trying to clean up here is getting away from us – to the Yanks, the Frogs, the Italians. But especially to the Spanish, would you believe? Our General over here doesn't want their generals over there to get annoyed about the deluge, so we're going to go over and keep an eye on what our riff-raff is getting up to in the mother country. You're going to carry out the same little job you've been doing for me here, but in Madrid. Pay attention, learn to recognize the signs, be discreet, raise the alarm. You'll have to listen hard, because I don't know what they speak over there, but it isn't Spanish.* And he roars with laughter.

Madrid was the ideal place for me, being both hard and welcoming at the same time, like a sort of boarding school. The prevailing atmosphere of suspicion suited me. Somehow the work was easier. My boss, in the company where I was supposedly working (and where I passed myself off as an impecunious exile, like the others), was an absentminded old man who spent his nights watching Sarita Montiel films. The true authority was a spare and silent Murcian, from the Ministry of the Interior, who had been with the Generalísimo in Africa. I saw him only half a dozen times, and on each occasion he made the same observation. *Everything's going well, very well. Keep it up.*

That banal belief in time healing all wounds is wrong-headed: we grow accustomed to our wounds, which is not the same thing. So it was that, at an earthy forty-something, I felt able to accept the advances of the refined Quita, without fearing that she would usurp that other person, both absent and irreplaceable. Quita found me amusing, intriguing, I was her *gentleman*, she would say, when we were together. *My Dark Blanca*, I would reply. I would never have made the first move. It was she who approached me, her glasses shining, her mouth always on the point of a smile, a tremulous down on her lips. She was generous, more than she ought to have been to me, the false victim, the lying lover, impostor in everything.

Now there is a sort of phosphoresence in the fog, a vaguely luminous darkness, a dirty light. I move forward. I hear the voice of Quita, cajoling, begging me to stay with her, not to leave her. There is something obscene, grotesque, in hearing loving words from someone we do not love. We suddenly notice the spittle in the corners of their mouth, a broken vein on their nose, sleep on the lashes they are so coquettishly seeking to flutter. Quita's voice goes on and on, and I move farther and farther.

I want it to disappear: her, her voice, her face, her hands. But she continues to whine in this mist, her whining becomes mingled with the yelping of the bitches, her teeth with their fangs, her red fingernails with their claws. I would like to set them on him, this pack of animals and women. On him I would like to set loose all these piebald creatures with their flaming eyes. On him I unleash my furies, but to no avail. All I can do is advance, without feeling that I am moving. As though I were walking in a circle which is growing ever tighter, a spiral in the centre of which I am doomed not to find the other, but myself, the man I once was, patiently waiting for the person I am now.

Forward.

Few of the refugees passing through the Martín Fierro centre really interested us. Most of them were poor bastards who had grudgingly taken flight, in the manner of a cat shooed from its home with a broom. Others, who had once been fighters, now appeared dull and sterile, incapable of the slightest protest. A few had been transformed, or were in the process of transforming themselves into obedient members of the bourgeoisie, regretting their youthful ethos, willing to put all that behind them. These got transferred to the credit column. But there were also some in debit. The ones who were still raging. The ones who demanded reparation, public vengeance, future justice. The ones who gathered testimonials, confessions, private statistics. The ones who probed memories. Those who ascribed to themselves the role of recording angels. They were the ones who had to be watched, whose names were kept on file.

Like any offical job, there is a bureaucracy involved in denunciation. At the top of the tree are the anonymous men who make the initial and final decisions, who have no private lives, the initiators of public action, the masters of history. Their subordinates are the ones who communicate orders, who appear to be important, who have personalities, names, ranks. Beneath them are the ones who execute the orders, who mete out the blows, who pull the trigger. Finally come the underlings, the ones who use their ears, open their eyes, make notes, who live on surveillance and indiscretion. I am one of these last. I watch, listen and tell. Perhaps that is the reason why I no longer have ears, eyes, a voice. Nothing exists outside my mind. While yours is occupied with dreams of me.

One day, at Blanca's office, I see him. I recognize him. It's his face, his frighteningly fine-featured face. He has the looks of a soap star, of an actor in a commercial, a face at once dreamy and astute, a face that looms over the piles of books at the Martín Fierro like an enormous harvest moon. There it is, implacable, stuck in my eyes like a shard of glass, that face which is also a thousand faces, all the same, all calm and smiling, all the faces the face over which she bent, solicitously, bathing his bloodied ear. There he is, that day when Blanca asked me to drop into her office and pointed to the man standing beside the bookcase, like one of those scabby old statues of Chinese clay. There he was, waiting for me, as I had waited for him since that afternoon. We shook hands. While he introduced himself I was thinking: *How can I make him suffer?*

During the months that followed, our paths inevitably crossed many times. Images of him keep repeating themselves: in the café, in the street, at the Martín Fierro, at the exit of a theatre, at a gathering of literary friends. We saw each other at meetings, soirées, in the street on summer evenings, in cafés during the winter, a word here, a greeting there, never anything that would give away the secret intimacy we shared, our past history. We are undisclosed rivals – he doesn't know it, and I can't forget it. And while the image of her disappears, his reaffirms itself, multiplying itself, as though in a corridor of crystal-clear mirrors.

Let's get technical. The needle on a lie detector traces onto sheets of rolling paper a zig-zag line that seems never to commit itself either way: only in the moment of an absolute truth will the line become firmer, clearer. That unbroken, straight line is also the one made by a encephalogram when a patient dies. You have to keep an eye on both of them during an interrogation: they never both show the same state. To get to the truth without ending the life is our aim – that was my job. My first encounters with him were all about following the line of the lie-detector needle; now I'm after the other kind, the straight line, the inevitable one.

Every scene is acted out with protagonists and minor figures who flit on and off stage. The ridiculous Berens, the clown, the rhymester. A certain disgusting Cuban, either a thief or an intellectual, I don't know which is worse. The Cuban's wife – I threatened her once, to get him to talk. The midwife, Camilo Urquieta, who brings inky abortions into the world.

Anonymous friends. Indispensable enemies. One or other passionate lady. Little acolytes. Choirboys. Maenads.

Women have always felt sorry for me. That isn't a good basis for passionate love, which is what I, the frustrated poet, have always sought after. The literature I once tried to write betrayed me pitilessly; it's better that way – less embarrassing. Women consoled me when I wanted them to die for me, an asp to the breast. It's cold comfort, like a sick man who knows that the lover sitting at his bedside, she who tenderly moistens his parched lips, will go out at the end of visiting time and throw herself into another man's arms.

He, on the other hand, elicited their love without even trying to win it. *Why?* I ask. Only little Andrea managed to keep him at her side. You should have seen her boasting about it. *He's at my place, we eat lunch together, we share a bathroom, we wake up together.* Andrea, for whom he was like an extremely rare edition of an important and famous book.

I bided my time.

Waiting is an art. You can study it, practise it. I observed, made notes, preparing reports and forecasts. I heard the Murcian say one day: *Gorostiza has an African patience.* I understood what he meant. Like the Sphinx. Like the pyramids. Made of sand.

Then we come to *In Praise of Lying*. It's a pathetic piece of work. I read it, of course. Incredulous at so much idiotic adulation, furious at literature's great priests and with the futile satisfaction of knowing that my enemy had failed. As a book, *In Praise of Lying* is pompous, colourless and spent. How can people have said, many times over, that this is a masterpiece? I listened to their ravings without advancing an opinion. Because, who would have paid any attention to me, who would have listened to my criticism, in the midst of that choir of fulsome, stupid angels?

The rest is trivial: the author's adventures, the story of the publication, the public adoration. My protests would have counted for nothing. The book exists now, as a planet or a river exists, indifferent to those who travel over one or drown in the other. *In Praise of Lying* has a place outside our meagre lifespan. They've dubbed it an "immortal work". It is to be an immortal work, to my great chagrin. The earth is flat, and the sun revolves around it.

But not the man himself. He had to be crushed, like a stinking pile of waste, dissolved in a sewer. And I had the means. I had compiled quite a promising dossier on him. It would be enough to attack him. A mere formality. Once apprised of the man's past enormities, albeit fabricated, the Murcian would give his approval. What better moment than the very day of his artistic coronation! My invitation to the launch arrived, with some unctious drivel in Urquieta's hand. I went along early.

The file we held on the Antonio Machado was dense. Prohibited books. Censored magazines. Obscene authors. Readers who have no decency either in politics or pornography. Information withheld from customs, the police, the church. Objectionable comings and goings. Unacceptable conversations and even readings. All that arrogant intelligentsia which likes to call itself "enlightened". All their hangers-on too. Something had to be done.

One day the Murcian tells me to go and see the results for myself. I arrive early in the morning. The bookshop's front is burnt out, the window smashed. Black pages flutter in the air and a handful of curious passers-by are trying to make out any words that remain. Inside the premises, there isn't much damage. There are still piles of books on the tables or stacked on the shelves, all of it covered with a dusting of ash. *It's not that bad*, I think, seeing a woman standing in the doorway, crying. *Who are the animals that did this?* asks a man in a white shirt. *They are the Warriors of Christ the King*, I think of telling him. *They're a bunch of pretentious bastards anyway, God's booksellers*. I would have liked to tell those idiots that you achieve nothing with a paltry gesture like this. As if anyone cares about a few kids getting excited over slim volumes of poetry. I spot one singed cover and try to remember some verses I thought I had forgotten. A fruitless endeavour. I go over to the woman and ask if I can help her. She says nothing, so I start picking up some of the books that were sent flying by the explosion. I take one away in my pocket. As a memento.

I'm having lunch with Quita one afternoon when she tells me that tomorrow we're going to a launch. I guess which one it is. She mentions the book. She names the author. I watch as her mouth grinds the meat, the down on her lip glistening with grease. I can't stand seeing her eat. She breaks the bread with her hands, puts a piece in her mouth, mentions his name again and it's as if she were swallowing phlegm. Then she picks up an apple and takes a bite out of it, and a mixture of foam and spit forms at the corners of her mouth. She crunches up the fruit vigorously, while talking about the next day's event and, when she opens her mouth, I can see a great, white bubble floating over her pink-brown tongue. She talks and eats, eats and talks. Quita, who had a horror of silence, disappears now into the mist.

Two figures rise up like columns, winding around one another, her and him, the ones that matter.

They appear, growing larger in front of my eyes, in front of what would have been my eyes if I could see. He, with his spurned retinue of women, he who wanted to be with her, he who was chosen by her. They remain there, erect, united, two in one. Because, even when she is no longer there, she is still with him. I can't manage to detach them.

Onwards.

The presentation, a ceremony to honour his book. The book he wrote. The idiots talk to him, men admire him, women desire and protect him. He is silent, like a king. Why speak, when the world rushes to celebrate you? Almost without surprise, among the crowd I spot my Cuban and his wife – she of the ubiquitous hat, she who ought to be dead. If I can manage to corner the three of them, what a ceremony I'd prepare, what a presentation, what a bonfire for the Devil and Christ the King.

Him, at the front. Him, still not saying a word. Him, suddenly frightened. Him, running towards the street. Everyone perplexed, astonished, embarrassed. I decide to follow him. He comes to a door. He goes in. I see a light go on. I wait. The Cuban and the hat woman arrive. Quita arrives, a flustered busybody. Quita comes out again, crying, poor cow. Then I decide to go in. I ring the bell. He answers the door. I step into the hall. We argue. I try to open the door behind him and he tries to stop me opening it. I see the repugnant Cuban. *Hello, Chancho*, I say, and I place my bag on a chair, as if this were a homecoming, a long-awaited return to a familiar place. *And hello, Señora*, I say to the resurrected one, his scrawny girlfriend.

The Cuban looks at me. I can't read his expression. The woman makes a face, somewhere between disparaging and flirtatious. We were about to leave, she says.

Sit down, I answer. Or I order her – it's all the same. And I tell them that I was about to ask the other one how they were planning to share out the money hidden in Switzerland. To make them aware of it, I suppose. To frighten them. To make him, my prey, quake.

But he pretends not to understand, he says he doesn't know what I'm talking about. I suggest he ask his fat friend for some explanations. In fact, it doesn't really matter to me whether he knows or not. That is not the guilt that interests me.

Then I feel as if I'm suffocating. I need air. I go to the balcony doors and fling them wide open. He tries to close them. I stop him. He struggles. Meanwhile the Cuban and his flamingo make their getaway, petrified, no doubt. Before leaving, they tell him that his book is very good. Even in these last words, they lie. Who cares. He doesn't even look at them. He's looking at me.

From the foggy depths, a pair of thin, hairy arms reach upwards. The arms encircle me and grow longer, wrapping around me. The arms become embedded in my body. Little roots burst out of the hands and grip my skin, sinking tiny tentacles, boring through the flesh to the bone's marrow. The arms envelop me and I have the impression of disappearing beneath their ramifications.

I want to open the balcony doors. He wants to close them. We struggle. A light goes on in one of the houses opposite. Then I gather all my strength and shake off his arm and I feel him swing himself over the balcony's low railing. A vacuum in the air, a fall that seems like a jump, and the horrible thud of a body dashed against the pavement. For a long moment I don't know whether it's him or me who has fallen.

I close the doors, pick up my bag, go out to the staircase and run. Up the dark street I run, almost without drawing a breath. At the top, in front of a lit-up theatre, I pause, euphoric. This is it, I tell myself, this is the end. He's not here any more, she's not here, only I am here, still standing, finally liberated, ready to begin again, the old skin shrugged off, scrubbed clean, back in the starting blocks, turning over a new leaf. *Because I won't ever run into him again,* I told myself, *because he's gone for ever.* He's out of reach now, in a place beyond the horizon that I can't make out, and which keeps retreating as I advance.

In Madrid, everything is cloaked in damp, as though the bricks themselves exhale it. At night, in the lamplight, the air turns rusty. I walked through the damp mist to my house, unable to distinguish the trees from the men. I reached my door, went upstairs and sat down at the table. I needed to get some sleep before the morning came, and everything changed.

I poured myself a large glass of Urquieta's sherry. And then another. And one more. I finished the bottle and started on the other. Urquieta had been kind enough to open them before the event began, so that the public could help themselves. But there had been no event. The star had fled. What shame she would have felt to witness the flight of her pusillanimous paladin. What remorse, what anguish. Now I was the artist, the victorious hero, the flame, the beau. I felt what great actors must feel when the curtain falls after a stellar performance. A rejuvenating exhaustion, an overwhelming euphoria. A lump in the throat.

A burning. A drowning. Something claws at the back of my throat, ripping the veins, tearing into the flesh. Everything is fire, everything is smoke. I need water, air. Now my guts are bursting into flames. Beneath the nails, my fingers are glowing red, black. My lungs struggle like two great headless birds, their scaly wings thrashing to survive. Nothing can fill them, nothing but blood that is warm as lava. I want to stop the invasion, the burning; it has to stop, such a pain cannot continue, it's an animal devouring me from the inside, drowning me in sand, mud, blood.

It's impossible to shout, impossible to give a voice to this extreme agony. So much pain doesn't fit into this crumbling flesh, this shattering head, these limbs which are falling to pieces and turning into embers. I feel my face falling off in chunks, my skin peeled off alive, my organs hurled at my feet. I am coming apart, but the pain remains. I am disappearing in a storm of burning ashes.

Then suddenly, there is no pain. There is no body. There is nothing, except the contents of my memory.

I want my dreamer to wake up. For this to be over.

I see nothing.

I hear nothing.

I feel...

5

FRAGMENTS

"If God offered me, in His right hand, absolute truth and, in His left hand, only the quest for truth, stipulating that I should always fail in that quest, and if He said to me *choose!*, I would humbly take His left hand and say *Father, give me this one! Absolute truth belongs only to You.*"

Gotthold Ephraim Lessing
Wolfenbüttler Fragmente

The story ends here. The true reader has no need to pursue this any further. This is it. All that matters has been said. To know who killed whom, how and why are questions that interest only bureaucrats or the police inspector, and they will not read these pages. The character I came to know through other voices is almost inexistent; he travels from hypothesis to hypothesis depending on the fit of his profile with certain data and preconceptions. His appearance changes like one of those garden statues which alter imperceptibly as the light changes during the day. But this, as a truth, is inadmissible. It isn't even journalism.

And although my vocation may be modest, there is no reason not to follow it faithfully. Not all those different Bevilacquas are the ones pursued by the journalist. Not all the facets of a reality interest him. Only one, if he is sincere, or perhaps none. That is why he writes. To show things from one particular, personal point of view. Now I think that it was that desire that prompted me to be a journalist. To see my name at the foot of a column of newsprint. To declare my ownership. To say what I feel, what I believe. To give my vision of a world that secretly enthralls me.

Perhaps that is what defines a journalist, rather than the false objectivity we're supposed to take pride in. My grandfather, who escaped from the war, used to tell me to look at the dark underside of stones, where the hardness yields to earth, moss and insects. My grandfather was Spanish, from a coastal town I shall never visit called Sant Feliu de Guíxols. My father forbade us to ask our grandfather about those years, but my sister and I used to whisper in his ear "Grandpa, did you kill anyone in the war?" or "Grandpa, is it true that you had to eat rats or die of hunger?" And he would smile and say "yes" to everything. My father had brought him to live with us after my grandmother's death, because he had tried to end his life twice. We never left him alone.

In spite of being with him all the time, we knew very little about his life. Then two years ago, by chance, thanks to an old teacher from the Victor Hugo High School, I discovered the reason why he had come to Poitiers. When he heard my name, this teacher told me that he had known a Terradillos in 1939, during the years of Spanish exile, when they were both about eighteen years old. I found out then that my grandfather had worked as a builder in Barcelona, and that he had joined a group of Franco's Nationalists, though I don't know under what circumstances. I don't believe, however, that my grandfather had any real political convictions. I imagine that he was drawn in by strong voices, easy dogma and a certain superstitious faith that accompanied him to the end of his life, prompting him to make the sign of the cross every time he walked past a church.

When it was known that the Nationalists were about to enter the city, my grandfather and his friends came out of their hiding places and waited, like victors, at the Hospital Clínico where, miraculously, they managed to get hold of meat, sausages and wine. For weeks they had been eating nothing but rice. My grandfather drank himself into oblivion.

The next morning, he woke up almost naked, in a garden behind the hospital. A long procession was slowly moving past, some people on foot, others in carts pulled by mules, or carried by their companions. At first, in his dazed state, he thought that these were the Nationalists arriving. Almost immediately, he realized that they were Republicans, fleeing towards the border. He was frightened that they might recognize him, so he draped himself with a blanket and joined them. The distance between Barcelona and the French border is not great – to my grandfather it must have seemed interminable.

When they finally saw the French soldiers coming to meet them, those that had held on to their weapons threw them onto the ground. The French boiled up milk in great earthenware jugs and, as the Spaniards passed by, gave each one a steaming mug and a hunk of bread. The men were separated from the women and children, and sent to different refugee camps. My grandfather did as he was instructed.

That night he began to cough and struggle for breath. A French nurse recognized the symptoms of pneumonia and asked him his name. My grandfather told him and, with an insistence that must have seemed suspicious, claimed to have belonged to one of the International Brigades which, before their disbandment in the autumn of 1938 (so the teacher told me) had been led almost exclusively by Spaniards. Without batting an eyelid, the nurse, who was no older than my grandfather, noted down the information in an official document. Weeks later, under his new identity of Republican refugee, my grandfather was taken out of the border camp and sent to a centre close to Poitiers. There he met my grandmother, who was working on one of the surrounding farms. My father was born three years later.

My grandmother's and the teacher's families were neighbours, and the story of the recent arrival was shared, but kept quiet. Poitiers has a long tradition of secret stories, doubtless since that morning when Charles Martel vanquished the Moorish army and dozens of exhausted men put down Moorish roots to become Moreau and Morisette.

I don't know if such approximations explain who we are. I don't know if my grandfather's story is to blame for my interest in the doubtful, in the indefinable, the ambiguous aspects of certain personalities. What is true is that I was going to write the story of Alejandro Bevilacqua as a multi-faceted character whose many parts would be converted, through my reading, into one Bevilacqua, coherent and my own.

When I first thought of writing about his case, I imagined a long, complex, well-documented essay, a biography with novelistic touches for the sensitive reader and essayistic asides for the more erudite. My intention was to compose an anecdotal portrait of that mysterious man which would go back to his origins in La Rochelle at the end of the nineteenth century, and which would detail the saga of the Guitton family, of the little girl, Mariette, of the arduous journey from Europe to South America, of their meeting with the provincial Bevilacquas, ending, hundreds of pages later, with the publication of the masterpiece and the death of the false author.

But that was before. Now that I know (or believe I know) the story of Alejandro Bevilacqua, I also know that I shall never write it.

Partly because it does not exist as a story, as something that the readers of *In Praise of Lying* might be looking for – a prologue or coda to this phantom book, a biography of that almost anonymous spectre, usurper of the author's role in the libraries of our world. Partly, also, because I fear not doing it justice, through a lack of skill and intelligence. Partly, finally, because, even if I could do so, I would never know which of the versions that have come to me, including the combination of them all, is the real one.

This is the paradox that overwhelms me. An honest journalist (if there is such a thing) knows that he cannot tell the whole truth: the most he can aspire to is a semblance of truth, told in such a way as to seem real. In order to achieve that, a biography must give the impression of being incomplete, stopping before it reaches the final page, refusing to reach a conclusion. But, even if in real life we accept that our impressions are uncomfortably vague and inconsistent, in a journalistic book, especially one that pretends to depict a man of flesh and blood, such a timid style would be unacceptable.

Any good student (at least, any student from the Victor Hugo School) knows that the general theory of relativity explains all the major questions of the universe, out there where matter bends space and time. Quantum theory explains the small stuff, where matter and energy divide into infinitesimal particles. In their different areas, both theories are immensely useful. But if we attempt to use them together, they are shown to be absolutely incompatible. We lack one solid theory capable of explaining the world in its totality. So, how could I propose one that could completely account for that little piece of the world that was Alejandro Bevilacqua?

But my reasons are not merely literary and scientific. There is another, deeper and more intimate reason. I'll explain what I mean.

I have always liked toys, old toys above all. Things made of wood, with their cubes, arches and columns painted in faded red and green; little lead animals, pleasingly weighty in the hand, placed in lines on the rug; the noble game of snakes and ladders with its dizzying climbs and falls; the fantastic tumbler doll which seems to defy the law of gravity; the kaleidoscopes which try to give coherence to a fragmented and luminous cosmology. My grandfather used to find these rare and loveable objects, made by pensioners in their long afternoons at the sawmill, in shops that have long since disappeared; he never tried to tempt me with flashier toys.

One toy in particular has always fascinated me – a sort of puzzle called a Tangram. It came in a small, square box, on the lid of which was a Chinese-style landscape. The game consisted of seven geometric pieces in black Bakelite which one had to arrange on a squared paper template, where shaded areas depicted various figures: a mandarin, a rabbit, a tower, a lady with a parasol. It looked easy, but it wasn't. The outlined shapes had to be covered precisely with the black pieces. I rarely succeeded in matching the two exactly.

Bevilacqua's case was one of the times I failed. I can perfectly see the shaded silhouette of the man in my imagination, but I still need one or two pieces of information to cover it all. No matter how I reorganize the testimonies, however I try to trim them or turn them around, there is always one which does not fit with the others, which overlaps or doesn't meet what I would call the exact version.

Of course it isn't the first time I've failed in an investigation of this kind. And on such occasions a journalist worth his salt should know how to concede defeat. There is no shame in defeat. It doesn't hurt me to admit it: a faithful portrait of Alejandro Bevilacqua is going to require more skilful hands than mine.

If, however, I were obliged to defend my case, or to justify my attempt at depicting a figure like him, so mysterious and sombre, I would say that, other-worldly as he was, Bevilacqua embodied for me a certain human spontaneity. Nothing heroic or intrepid, nor even passionate, but something less pompous, more commonplace. A quality that falls somewhere between equivocation and desire, between the things we say accidentally and what we contrive to say. Not lies, which require deliberation and skill, along with a recognition of the truth in order to betray it. It's something more serious, more tragic and subtle, more essential. This quality I'm talking about is the same one which, on hot afternoons, makes the asphalt shimmer like water, or which prompts us to put a hand on the shoulder of a woman whose back reminds us of a long-lost friend, or which leads us up to a flat we believe is ours, to knock on a door behind which an unknown person is about to take some irreparable step.

I've said that I'm looking for, or was looking for, a singular, exact version. Perhaps, in the case of Bevilacqua, that version was unwittingly revealed by one of the various witnesses to his life who confided in me. But, in order to recognize it, I (whether journalist or confessor) would need to be capable of identifying it, of knowing beforehand which are these qualities, like a blind man intuiting the shades of a certain colour or a deaf man the tonality of a piece of music. I mean: I would need to know who Bevilacqua was before I could know whether the portrait offered me is authentic or not.

I'll go further. I don't know whether Bevilacqua himself would have recognized, in that series of biographical versions, which one was his, the real one. How can one know, among all the various faces reflected back to us by mirrors, which one represents us most faithfully and which one deceives us? From our tiny point in the world, how can we observe ourselves without false perceptions? How can we distinguish reality from desire?

During my childhood in Poitiers, I was once witness to an event that sheds a mysterious light – at least for me – on this dilemma. My parents, my sister, my grandfather and I lived close to the Parc de Blossac, in one of the developments built there in the 1970s, at the foot of the Tour-à-l'Oiseau; my school was close by, just before the Pont Saint-Cyprien, by the river Clain. A good part of the route from my house to school ran alongside a narrow stretch of the river. My grandfather – who, in spite of his advanced years, often accompanied me – was walking ahead of me that morning. The spring rains had swollen the river, which threatened to flood the hideaways of dozens of mangy cats. Suddenly, as we reached the site of the old sawmill, I saw my grandfather give a brief shrug and throw himself into the water. I could not shout or move. People near the river raised the alarm, fetching a gendarme who lived close by. I remember him perfectly. He was a tall, thin man who moved slowly, always dressed in an impeccably neat uniform. He walked on to the river bank, took his gun out of the halter and, pointing it at the would-be suicide, shouted: "Get out of there or I'll shoot!" My grandfather obeyed and we returned home, he dripping water and I terrified, both of us silent. Bevilacqua, I believe, would also have obeyed.

I've decided not to write a profile of Bevilacqua. Lover, hero, friend, victim, traitor, apocryphal author, accidental suicide and so much more: that's a lot of things for one man. I'm all too aware of my limitations. And at the same time, I feel that the very fact of resigning myself to not writing has imbued my character with new life: Bevilacqua has declared himself. With my act of resignation, Bevilacqua steps forward with a body, a voice, a presence. It is I, his reader, his hopeful chronicler, Jean-Luc Terradillos, who disappears.

Thanks to: Vanesa Cañete, Javier Cercas, Valeria Ciompi, Marusha and Tony Díaz, Silvia Di Segni, Graeme Gibson, Maite Gallego, Felicidad Orquín, Enrique López Sánchez, Willie Schavelzon, Gudrun Schöne-Tamisier, Zoe Valdés.

BORN IN BUENOS AIRES IN 1948, ALBERTO MANGUEL is a Canadian writer, translator and editor. He is the author of numerous non-fiction books such as *The Dictionary of Imaginary Places* (co-written with Gianni Guadalupi in 1980), *A History of Reading* (1996), *The Library at Night* (2007) and *Homer's Iliad and Odyssey: A Biography* (2008), and novels such as *News from a Foreign Country Came* (1991), for which he won the McKitterick Prize.

www.almabooks.com